THE GODFATHER IV

ALI ZOHDI

Made with ❤ on the Notion Press Platform
www.notionpress.com

I would like to extend my deepest gratitude to certain individuals who played a crucial role in my life, i.e. I would have never made it without their guidance and support. My university professors Dr. Mona Elnamoury , Dr. Amira Elzikrd & Dr. Mustafa Riad at MSA University.

My dearest mentor Ms. Dina Lamey at AUC (Amercian University in Cairo), who truly believed in my talent, and significantly helped me to nourish it. Words can never describe how much I love you.

Last but far from least, my father Dr. Ahmed Zohdi, no matter how much I wrote to thank you I will never ever be able to return even 1% of all the things you have done for me ever since I came to this world.

There is an endless list of people, to whom I would like to express my eternal indebtedness, a list in fact that will be as lengthy as the novel I wrote...

Thank you, and I love you all.

Contents

Preface

In the middle of the journey of our life I came to myself
within a dark wood where the straight way was lost.
Dante Alighieri

CHAPTER ONE

UNKNOWN FATE

On a cold, bitter January night in 1985, Manhattan was wrapped in a cloak of snow and silence, as the icy wind rattled the hospital windows like loose bones. Inside Bellevue Hospital, its sterile corridors whirring faintly with the rhythm of machines and muffled footsteps, Claudia Soleri lay in the maternity ward, her body exhausted, her soul trembling with both relief and dread. Bellevue was no ordinary hospital; it was older than the country itself. Founded in 1736, it is the oldest public hospital in the United States, its history woven deep into the city's veins. It had seen soldiers carried from battlefields, waves of immigrants struck by plagues, addicts, lunatics, paupers, and the forgotten... The building where Claudia now rested; the towering, twenty-five-story "Cube" along the East River, was only a decade old, a state-of-the-art fortress of medicine. Yet for all its modern walls, its gleaming halls, its reputation, it could not shield her from the gravity of what she had just brought into the world. At twenty-five, she had given birth to her first and only child. A small and fragile son already bearing the massive burden of two generations of grief. An infant whose life, as fate would decree, would one day alter not only his own destiny, but the lives of everyone who crossed his path...

As Claudia lay there, fighting the heaviness in her eyelids, the fluorescent light buzzed overhead. She closed her eyes, and in that humming silence the sharp, mournful past came rushing back, unbidden, fragments of an orphan's life. She was only seven when her father was taken from her. The day was Friday, May 19, 1967, etched into her heart like an indelible scar. She remembered the sound of her school shoes on the worn stairwell of their Mulberry Street apartment, the scent of marinara sauce drifting faintly from some neighbor's kitchen, and then two Army officers waiting outside her door. Their expressions were rigid, their eyes heavy with a sorrow they had long since learned to disguise. One bent down, stroked her cheek softly, and walked away without a word. Inside, her mother, Maria, sat petrified on the sofa, a still statue of despair. Claudia, sensing the shift in the air, whispered, "What's wrong, Mommy?" "Daddy got killed in the war," Maria said, her voice unflinchingly calm, as if any trace of gentleness would have shattered her into pieces. Then came the tears; the wailing storm of a child and a widow, two voices braided in inconceivable agony. The officers, already retreating down the stairs, heard the cries echoing after them. By then, such sounds were no novelty; they were part of the Vietnam War's rancorous soundtrack. Claudia's father, Robert Soleri, had died in a grenade blast. His body had been torn to pieces, leaving nothing to bring home; no flag-draped coffin, no military honors. His sacrifice was swallowed whole by a war that gave back absolutely nothing; no recognition, no dignity, not even a grave for his wife and child to lament at.

Robert Soleri had never been destined for glory, and certainly he had been no soldier by choice. A poor second-generation Italian-American, he had worked long hours as a waiter at Denari's, a Brooklyn restaurant frequented by wiseguys and neighborhood toughs. He had been clever, mild, good with customers, the kind of man whose demeanor earned him favor with everyone, especially the owner, Nicholas "Nicky Glasses" Denari.

But Robert was poor, the son of Italian immigrants in a city that still spat at their kind. He had no connections, no college degree, no shield from the draft. And being Italian meant carrying a burden of suspicion, a shadow of criminality cast by men with names like his. He worked nights, trudging home under streetlamps where the cops prowled. To them, his dark eyes and accent marked him as suspect. "Where you going so late, huh? You some kind of tough guy?" Even before Vietnam claimed him, America had marked him. One night in November 1964, it went too far... Claudia would never forget the story Maria told her of that foreboding night when Robert, walking home late from his shift, was stopped by two cops. One, Officer Russo, an Italian-American himself, had sneered at Robert's nose, as well as his dark eyes, and then hurled a slur. Officer Russo stopped him, eyed him with disdain. "Christ, at first I thought he was a fucking kike. Look at this nose, these eyes..." Robert contemptuously muttered *"Disgrazia"*. Disgrace.

The word alone was more than enough to set Russo off; he snapped, his flashlight arcing through the air before smashing into Robert's face. Bone cracked, skin split, blood poured his face. Robert went down, while humiliation had sunk into his soul. He regained consciousness in a cell, charged with resisting arrest, facing years of incarceration for nothing. If it had not been for Nicky; Robert's employer, friend, and, in ways his unspoken protector, Robert might have lost years of his life behind bars. Nicky pulled strings, called in favors, and finally got him released. A couple of days later, Robert walked free, his nose broken, his dignity fragmented, but even that *clemency* came with a bitter lesson: in America, men like Robert were absolutely nobodies.

Outside the precinct, Robert asked the question that kept burning inside him like a volcano waiting to erupt: "What's going to happen to that animal who did this to me?" Nicky sighed, adjusting his glasses. "You expect a cop to pay for beating an Italian waiter? You should be kissing their asses for letting you walk out, kid. Look, I know this sounds tough; don't ask for justice where it doesn't live." He tucked a hundred-dollar bill into Robert's pocket. "Take the week off. Go home to your wife. Count your blessings." Robert said nothing. He just watched Nicky disappear into the crowd, the world shrinking around him.

They had been, for the most part, a happy couple, Robert and Maria, bound by a quiet contentment that money could not buy. Arguments were rare; grievances were small and polite. He waited tables. She stitched garments with nimble, patient hands. They lived modestly, but their poverty never eroded the small rituals that made a home; a shared cup of coffee before dawn, the way Maria hummed as she fed the sewing machine, the soft laugh they traded over a burned dinner. What made their lives luminous, though, was Claudia. Their daughter was the single bright thing between them, the long-awaited answer to five years of emptiness. For half a decade they had moved from one doctor to another, hopeful for an explanation, for a cure, and always coming away with the same baffling verdict; two healthy bodies, and yet no child. The waiting drained the color from their evenings and bred a private frustration that sat in their throats like swallowed smoke. Still, when the miracle finally came, it felt like vindication. God, fate, fortune, call it what you will, had delivered.

"She's so beautiful, and terribly smart," Robert would say, pride cracking his voice. "Who knows? Maybe she'll be the first woman president of the United States." The claim was half joke, half prophecy; both parents wrapped themselves in hopeful imaginings for Claudia's future. They pinned their ambitions on her small shoulders like medals. Robert adored his daughter. He never denied her anything he could afford, and he measured his sacrifices in the hours he logged for her sake. He worked like a man trying to buy time; sixteen, sometimes eighteen hours a day, weekends swallowed whole by shifts and tips. Mornings found him stumbling into the city before dawn, evenings enveloped him in a weary stillness long after the streetlamps blinked out. More often than not, their encounters were flashes; a hurried kiss as she left for school, a tired wave as she returned from hers. Brief, stray moments that kept them tethered but never close. Guilt weighed on him as heavily as his work-broken back. He told himself he labored so Claudia would have more than he had; a life without want, a chance he never got. Yet every dollar earned felt like a small theft of the one thing he could not buy back; time with his child. "Life is a bitch," he liked to mutter to himself, a private joke in defiance of desperation. At least, he would add, it was bearable. Then came the incident. A few days ago, something happened that shifted everything; an affront that placed him on the edge of a precipice and cast the future he had fought so hard to secure into doubt. For the first time, the arithmetic of sacrifice and reward failed to add up, and Robert found his family, his very life, suddenly at stake.

From that night on, Robert Soleri was never the same again. He still worked, those overextended hours between the restaurant and a grocery store, but he carried his shame like a shroud. He withdrew from friends, from his wife, from life itself. He refused invitations, never joined festivals, lived only to provide for his daughter. Even Maria's tireless efforts; her cooking, her tenderness, and most of all, her desperate embrace in bed, could not heal what had been broken... She could see the storm still raging inside her husband. The bruises on Robert's face were only the surface; what truly ached lay far deeper, in places no ice pack could reach. Still, she tried... Tenderly she dabbed at the cuts, pressed cold compresses against the swelling, and kissed the raw edges of his pain as if her lips alone might heal them. She cooked his favorite lasagna, filling their small home with the scent of simmered tomatoes and baked cheese, hoping the familiar comfort might soften the hardness in his eyes. Later, when the night grew quiet and little Claudia was asleep, Maria slipped into her light-brown nightgown; the one that caught the lamplight and clung to her curves, and gave herself over to him with every ounce of devotion she knew how to summon. It was never just one role Maria played. She had a gift, almost theatrical in its breadth; mother, housekeeper, confidante, lover. She moved between them with a grace that felt instinctive, as if generations of Italian women had handed her this inheritance; the art of being everything for the man she loved. And on most nights, her performance was enough. Enough to soothe, to lift, to remind Robert that the world could still be kind in the privacy of their bed.

But not this time.

Her caresses, her cooking, her laughter, even her body seemed to glance off him like rain against stone. The humiliation he had endured clung to him like a second skin, burrowed too deeply. No matter how fervently she tried to chase it away, it sat between them, an uninvited third presence in their marriage. For the first time, Maria's arsenal of tenderness and passion failed her. The plan, carefully woven from love and instinct, unraveled in her hands. One night, as Maria straddled her husband, she felt his energy falter. His hands, once eager to explore her body, now lay still. The intimacy between them was fading, replaced by a growing disquietude.

"What's wrong, Robert?" Maria asked softly as she slipped down beside him.

He remained silent.

"Talk to me, Robert..." she pressed, her voice tinged with irritation.

But he only stared at her, his silence heavy enough to drown the room. Tears welled in her eyes before he finally spoke, his voice breaking:

"What if Nicky couldn't save me? What would've happened to you and Claudia? How could I have survived in prison among such animals? Just because I'm Italian, they think I must be tied to the Mafia. Our heritage, Maria is our curse. We live in a society where no one takes our side, where nobody sympathizes when things go wrong, because of the reputation those thugs gave us. To them, being Italian, especially poor means you're trouble. An outlaw. A gangster. Tell me, Maria... do I look like a gangster to you? I don't know the first thing about that life. I've never even held a gun in my hands!"

Robert rose abruptly from the bed, lit a cigarette, and exhaled with trembling fury.

"How the hell am I supposed to live in a country where a mad police officer, who is also an Italian by the way, can brutalize me and walk away without punishment, without even an investigation? As if nothing happened! I was the one assaulted. I was the victim. And yet I had to apologize just to be set free. Is this America? Is this the land of opportunity our parents promised us? They lied to us, Maria. Or maybe they were fooled, the same way we were. I don't know... All I know is, I don't feel safe anymore. I'm terrified for Claudia. What if something else happens to me? What then? It's not right, Maria. None of it is right. I didn't deserve what happened to me!"

Maria watched him, stunned. She could barely process his words, but one thing became painfully clear; the man she had just made love to was no longer the same man she had married nearly ten years ago. Robert grew quieter, darker, a man hollowed out by fear of what might befall his family if fate turned cruel again; fear haunted him incessantly, leaving him incapable of inner peace... Fear of cops, fear of prison, fear of a society that saw his heritage as a curse. And when Vietnam came calling, he went without protest. For men like him, there had never really been a choice; even Nicky himself, with all his connections, could not have done *anything* about it...

Maria carried on as best she could, raising Claudia alone. But life's callousness had not yet finished with the poor girl, as new misfortunes emerged. At seventeen, Claudia was dealt another devastating blow from life's relentless hand; the tragic loss of her mother. Maria, an inveterate smoker, her slender fingers perpetually stained with nicotine; smoking a cigarette after a cigarette, each one burning the hours until sleep, eventually succumbed to lung cancer with terrifying swiftness. The tumor spread through

Maria's body like shards of a shattered vase embedding themselves deeper with every passing day. Claudia nursed her through nights of coughing and anguish, clinging to the hope that her mother might live long enough to see her graduate. Claudia, however, was slipping. Though sharp and gifted, her performance at school began to collapse under the weight of her mother's illness. Once a standout student, she now found it practically impossible to focus. "It breaks my heart, Claudia," said Mrs. Henderson, the principal of Brooklyn Technical High School, when she summoned her to the office. Her voice carried both warmth and urgency. "Someone with your potential should be winning scholarships not struggling to keep up. Look, I know what you're going through. Believe me, I've been through something similar myself. And I'm not saying it's easy. I know it's not. But you have to pull yourself together. You're capable of so much more. You can do a hell of a lot better, young lady. A hell of a lot."

From her earliest years, Claudia's brilliance had been indubitable. Teachers noticed it in kindergarten. By high school, her passion for math and physics set her apart, and her instructors spoke with unanimous conviction; she was destined for greatness, likely as an engineer. But fate had conspired against her. Her father's early death when she was just seven, the stifling indigence that defined her upbringing, the absence, despite Nicky's loyal support, of a stable family foundation, and now the cruelest blow of all; the looming, inescapable death of her mother. And by June of 1977, death befell. Claudia remembered the rasp of her mother's breath, the way Maria's eyes still burned with ferocity even as her body failed. She refused hospitalization, choosing instead to die in her own bed.

On her final night, Claudia heard her mother choking in the dark and rushed to her side. Maria's face was gaunt, her breath shallow, but her grip was fierce as she clutched her daughter's hand with the last of her strength. "Promise me, Claudia," she whispered. "Promise me you will never shame yourself. No drugs. No men who would dishonor you. Live with honor, Claudia; *onore*. Promise me." Claudia had nodded with blinding tears streaming down her face. "Please don't leave me mommy, please," Claudia repeatedly beseeched her mother. Then Maria's hand went limp. Claudia held it long after the warmth had faded, cherishing this moment of eternal farewell for as long as she could. Maria was gone; her pure soul wrested away by the implacable Big C, carried onward to face her merciful and equitable Creator, leaving her daughter with a single word echoing like a curse and a blessing in her heart: *ONORE*.

Years slipped quietly into one another; they unfolded like worn pages in a book no one noticed being read. Claudia struggled. She survived on grit and determination, her resilience the only armor life had left her. She worked, she fought, she endured. Nicky gave her a job at Denari's, and in that dim-lit restaurant of clinking glasses and whispered deals, her path crossed with destiny...

It was a late February afternoon in 1984, when the city air still carried the last bite of winter, but the streets beneath it signaled a blossoming spring to come. At Denari's Restaurant, the regulars began trickling in, shaking off the cold as they were greeted by Nicky with his usual charm. For nearly three decades, Nicky had made hospitality an art; a compliment here, a hand on the shoulder there, gestures that kept the guests feeling like family. Behind the counter, however, things were less smooth. The cash register had broken down that morning, leaving the young waitress to calculate every bill by hand. She leaned over her notepad, pen scratching across paper, brow furrowed in concentration. "Don't worry about it, boss," said Bob, the dishwasher, grinning as he carried a tub of plates to the back. "This girl's brain is like a goddamn calculator." Nicky walked over, patted her shoulder, and murmured with gratitude, "You saved my ass today, kid. Don't worry, I called the company. They'll send someone tomorrow to fix the machine."

"What about the bonus?" she asked without looking up, her tone serious.

"You don't have to worry about that either," Nicky assured her warmly before heading back to greet a new guest.

Bob lingered by the counter, smirking, curiosity glinting in his eyes. "So... how's Bryan? Haven't seen him around. He alright?" The girl shot him a sharp glance. "Get lost, Bob." Her reply cut through the air. Suddenly, the place fell eerily silent, forks frozen midair, conversations cut short, as the door swung open. A man entered, not tall, not imposing by sheer size, but carrying with him an authority that made the entire restaurant take notice. Two bodyguards flanked him, shadows with muscle. The man himself was in his late thirties, strikingly handsome in a tailored suit and tie. His dark eyes commanded attention, smoldering with a charisma that unsettled men and captivated women. Even the young waitress felt it instantly, as if a current had jolted through her. Nicky shot to his feet, respect radiating from every gesture. He clasped the man in a warm embrace, the kind of welcome that told everyone watching this was no ordinary guest. The room exhaled, conversations cautiously resumed, though all eyes stayed attuned to the newcomer.

"It's an honor to see you again, Godfather," Nicky said reverently. "Been too long. Anything I can do for you?" "For now," the man replied, his voice firm but gracious, "a table will suffice. I'm expecting company shortly."

"Of course, Godfather," Nicky acknowledged with the utmost decorum.

"Nicholas, get us a quiet spot. Somewhere private," the *guest* commanded.

"As you wish," Nicky said, bowing slightly before ushering him to a corner table. The bodyguards took position by the door, statuesque and watchful.

Nicky hurried back to the counter, whispering urgently to the waitress, "Drop what you're doing. Serve him yourself." She set her pen down, heartbeat quickening. Without a word, she adjusted her apron and moved toward the table, willing herself to appear calm though her eagerness betrayed her.

"What can I get you, Sir?" she asked politely.

He looked up at her. One glance was enough. Her beauty was arresting; dark hair pulled back neatly, hazel eyes luminous against a complexion touched by olive warmth. She wore no makeup, yet her face had a natural elegance, framed by an innocence that only heightened her allure. The apron could not disguise her figure, the curves that seemed to announce themselves with quiet defiance. She carried herself with grace that made it all the more striking.

"A glass of wine," he said, his tone almost casual.

"Red or white?" she asked, her lips curling into a playful smile.

He chuckled lightly. "I'm meeting with associates. You tell me, which is more suitable for business, red or white?"

She grinned, a little flustered. "Either works, I guess."

"Then red," he said. "Thank you."

The chemistry between them was undeniable. Nicky saw it, the other patrons felt it. The girl hurried off and returned with the glass, setting it before him with professional poise. Moments later, the door opened again. Two men entered; one short and heavyset, the other tall and wiry. There was a coarseness about them, something that prickled the atmosphere. Their curt greeting to Nicky did little to ease the tension. They moved directly toward the Godfather's table, answering his silent wave. They ordered coffee, but within minutes the shorter man's voice rose, loud and abrasive. The Godfather let it go once, then twice. On the third outburst, his fist came down on the table with a thunderous crack. The restaurant froze. Silence swept over the room. The short man swallowed hard, his words sinking to a mumble, scarcely audible to anyone beyond the table. Everyone now understood who held dominion in that place. The meeting ended quickly after that. The two men stood, offering deference before leaving, coffees untouched. The waitress, emboldened, stepped forward again.

"Anything else, Sir?" she asked gently.

"No, thank you," he replied, his composure restored.

"They didn't even finish their coffee. Was something wrong with it?" she asked, puzzled.

He smiled faintly. "No. They were simply in a hurry."

Reaching into his handmade leather wallet, he pulled out a crisp hundred-dollar bill and handed it to her. "Keep the change."

Her eyes widened. "Oh... that's too much, Sir. I can't... I mean, thank you. Thank you very much, Mr..."

"Corleone," he said smoothly. "Vincent Corleone. And you? What's your name?"

"Claudia," she whispered, almost breathless. "Claudia Soleri."

Bryan Stanley and Claudia Soleri had circled each other in an on-again, off-again storm of a relationship for nearly two years. Their story began one spring night in April 1982, at a house party on the Upper West Side hosted by Sophia Flamini; Claudia's childhood friend and, in many ways, her foil. Claudia and Sophia had first crossed paths back in junior high. Though Sophia never possessed even half of Claudia's quicksilver intelligence, she made up for it with charisma that could set a room alight. While Claudia shrank into her books, Sophia moved through adolescence like a general commanding troops, able to turn strangers into allies and adversaries into outcasts with nothing more than her wit and her tongue. Teachers who dared cross her found themselves besieged by a quiet revolt she would orchestrate in whispers and knowing glances. Her classmates called her *Mighty Sophie*; half in awe, half in fear. And yet, beneath the bravado, Sophia was Claudia's guardian angel. She defended the shy brunette from crude boys, from gossiping girls, from the sharp cruelties of youth. In return, Claudia lent her mind; helping Sophia through endless homework assignments, essays, and exams. It was a fair exchange; Sophia's protection for Claudia's brains, cementing a friendship that carried them beyond the walls of school and into adulthood. By the time Claudia walked into Sophia's party that fateful April night, she knew Sophia would already be surrounded by admirers. And there, leaning against the stereo, glass of cheap wine in hand, was Bryan Stanley.

Bryan was the sort of man who carried himself like an unfinished novel, always hinting at mastery that never quite materialized. He dressed well enough, though Claudia later learned half his wardrobe was borrowed. He spoke of painting with the fervor of a phenomenal genius wronged by the world, his eyes blazing with indignation at a society too venal to admit his so-called extraordinary *gift*. But in truth, Bryan was a drifter; a man in his mid-thirties who had never held a job longer than a season, never built a life, never grown roots. Women were drawn to him at first. He had the easy charm of a rogue, the grin of a man who could promise the world. But when the mask slipped, or rather, when they saw the drinking, the gambling, the lies, most fled. All but Claudia. She could not say why she stayed. It was not love; some deep instinct told her this was not the man her heart longed for. Yet she clung to him, as though by sheer will she could carve a partner out of this shapeless, selfish man. "Why don't you just dump this bum?!" Nicky barked at her one evening, after finding her in tears at the restaurant. To Claudia, Nicky was more than a boss; he was the closest thing to the father she had lost. But even with him, she could not confess the truth of her entanglement with Bryan. She only lowered her head and stayed silent.

Sophia was different. With Sophia, she could spill everything. The cheating, the gambling, the endless excuses. The worst of it was money; Bryan's constant stories about a sick mother, a struggling cousin with abandoned children, emergencies that always seemed to demand Claudia's small wages. Later, she would learn where that money really went; cheap motels, whores, and liquor.

"With the little I make from Nicky, I could barely make ends meet," Claudia sobbed to Sophia. "And he takes it and spends it on *them*. Can you imagine? Lies about his mother, about children, and all the while he's in bed with some whore."

"How do you even know?" Sophia asked, her tone sharp but protective.

"Nicky told me. And when I confronted him, Bryan couldn't even deny it."

Sophia's eyes narrowed with fury. "Let me talk to him. I'll straighten that bastard out."

But Claudia shook her head. "No. This is my problem. Mine to fix."

It was then she knew that Bryan Stanley was not the man she had been searching for. He was not reliable. He was not strong. He was not a man in the way her father had been; a steady anchor of warmth and sacrifice. Bryan was a shadow, and she had wasted too much light chasing him. And yet, even after that realization, the cycle continued. Bryan would reappear, full of apologies and promises, and Claudia would allow him back for a night, a week, only to send him away again. He never dared strike her. Perhaps because violence was not in him, or perhaps because Claudia's anger was a tempest few men could weather. Still, his betrayals carved something deep into her. This faltering, failed relationship scarred her trust, reshaped her vision, or rather, warped her perception of love. It left her vowing never to surrender her heart again, never to be deceived by a man's hollow promises. Until one evening, when a man named Vincent Corleone stepped into Denari's Restaurant, and with a single look, shattered that vow.

The door burst open with a muted squeak, and in stepped a doctor accompanied by a nurse with delicate, almond-shaped eyes. The scent of antiseptic adhered to their uniforms, sharp against the faint sweetness of baby powder that lingered in the maternity ward. "How are you doing now, Ms. Soleri? Do you remember me?" The doctor smiled warmly, her vowels polished by years in New York.

"I'm Dr. Anita Gupta, senior obstetrician here. I was the one who delivered your little prince." Claudia shifted against the hospital pillows, her body still heavy from the ordeal. She wanted to answer, to release the torrent of questions gathering inside her, but her throat felt thick. Sophie, perched protectively at her side, filled the silence with her own eager voice. "How is he?" she asked, her words tumbling out, bright with excitement. "He's doing well," Dr. Gupta assured, before glancing curiously toward Sophie. "And you must be...?" "I'm Sophia Flamini," she replied crisply. "Reporter at The New York Times, and Claudia's best friend." There was steel under her tone, as though she already anticipated the doctor's coming admonition. And it came. "I'm sorry, but visiting hours ended at eight. It's nearly ten now. Only first-degree relatives are allowed to stay." The doctor's voice was courteous but edged, clipped with authority. "I don't have any first-degree relatives," Claudia said quietly, her eyes dark with exhaustion. "This..." she gestured toward Sophie "is the only family I have." The room fell into a hush, thick as fog. Even the machines seemed to quiet, their beeps fading beneath the weight of her confession. Dr. Gupta cleared her throat gently, breaking the silence. "I don't want you worrying about anything, especially postpartum depression," she said, softening her tone. "If symptoms arise, they can be treated; medication, therapy. But not every woman experiences it. Everyone's journey is different. I'll be checking in on you after discharge, but for now, just focus on rest." Claudia gave a faint nod of gratitude. Sophie, however, kept her jaw clenched, her silence a shield against an argument she knew she could not win in this aseptic room. "Is there anything else I can do for you, Ms. Soleri?" "I want to see him." Claudia's voice, though weary, cut through the quiet with unexpected strength. For a fraction of a second, Dr. Gupta's eyes flicked toward Sophie, then back. A perfunctory smile. "Of course." She turned briskly and left.

Moments later, the nurse reappeared, rolling in a cradle that seemed almost too small, too fragile to hold such magnitude. Inside, swaddled in white, lay Claudia's son; his chest rising and falling with the soft rhythm of newborn dreams. Sophie gasped, her hand flying to her mouth. Claudia only stared, wide-eyed, as though the world had collapsed into that tiny bundle. Her tears came in a rush, breaking through the dam of equanimity in a flood no willpower could contain. Were they tears of joy, or grief, or fear? She could not tell. Perhaps all at once, or perhaps it did not even matter...

Memories of Maria pressed into her chest; her mother's absence louder than the storm that clattered the windows outside. She wished for her guidance, her hands, her voice. She wished the baby's father were here... But all she had was Sophie, and the fragile heartbeat of her son. Dr. Gupta excused herself with a polite goodbye, reminding Sophie once more that she could not stay long. When the door closed, Sophie grumbled under her breath, "Bitch," then bent over the cradle, unable to resist stroking the baby's downy cheek, kissing the tiny curled fists. "Where's Nicky?" she asked softly. "He's the one who brought me here yesterday," Claudia said, her tone edged with tenderness. "He stayed for hours, but I made him go home and rest. He'll pick me up tomorrow." "That's so sweet of him," Sophie murmured. She hesitated, then: "Does Bryan know?" Claudia's lips twisted. "Why would he even care?" Then she angrily continued. "He's probably off with one of his mistresses," pacing as though the words themselves burned her tongue. "I don't know... God, I really don't know anymore. One day he's literally on his knees, begging for forgiveness, swearing he deserves a second chance. But it's been over a year since we were truly *together*. A year." She stopped, her chest heaving, her hands trembling at her sides. "All I know is this Bryan cannot, and will not, play the father to my son. That charade ends now." Her voice broke into a low, resolute whisper. "I'm not alone anymore. I can't afford to be."

Sophie lowered her gaze, waited a beat, then pressed gently. "Aren't you going to tell his father?" Claudia's head snapped around, her eyes blazing. "Are you out of your fucking mind? Of course not!" "Relax," Sophie said quickly, hands raised. "You'll scare the baby. I was just asking." The baby stirred in Claudia's arms, and for a moment the anger dissolved into the hush of maternal instinct. Sophie, reading the shift, changed the subject.

"Have you chosen a name yet?"

Claudia gazed at her son, her voice quiet, steady. "Robert. Robert Soleri, Jr."

As the words left her lips, a deafening thunderclap split the January sky, hammering the windowpanes with a violence that seemed to seal the declaration in fate.

CHAPTER TWO

LOST LOVE

Don Vincent Corleone was not the kind of gangster one saw in the movies. He was no vulgar caricature spewing profanity, sneering at strangers, wallowing in sordid pleasures, or gunning men down on a whim. He had no patience for that asinine, cartoonish version of the mobster that television peddled to the masses. His world was darker, more complex; shaped by inheritance, tempered by loss, and sharpened by the lessons of those who came before him.

Yes, he had inherited the hot blood of his father, Santino. That quick temper, unchecked, had blurred Sonny's judgment and led him to a violent, macabre end. But Vincent had something Sonny never had; time and guidance. From his late uncle Michael, he learned how to master his rage. Michael had taught him that hatred was poison to judgment, that vengeance could not be the master of a man who sought to rule. From his uncle, he also learned a truth that weighed heavier than any crown; by accepting the mantle of Godfather, he had forfeited forever the hope of an ordinary life. But Vincent would never escape; he had chosen, or perhaps had been chosen, for a path carved in blood and shadow. He remembered well the words his uncle Michael spoke to him in Sicily, on the day he was proclaimed Don: *You won't be able to go back. You will be like me...* The words etched themselves into his soul. Yet even as he heard them, Vincent demanded power, demanded the authority to hold the family together. His ambition was iron-willed. He knew it would cost him, and it did. To consolidate his rule, he waged a ruthless war. He allowed no challenger to stand. One by one, he dismantled the rival families, ensuring that never again would a five-family structure rise to threaten the Corleones. This was the most invaluable of Michael's lessons: to cut danger out at the root, before it blossomed. But Vincent also understood something else; something Michael had grasped too late. Survival lay not only in bloodshed, but in legitimacy. Legitimacy became his shield and his weapon. He stepped carefully, using business to burnish his public image. He surrounded himself with intelligent, ambitious young men drawn from the upper stratum of society, men of education and pedigree who would be his emissaries to America's elite. Through them, he reshaped his persona, not as a thug in the shadows, but as a businessman, approachable, sociable, even charming, in the manner of his late grandfather, the legendary Don Vito Corleone, whose shadow still loomed over every corner of the family's empire, and always will... Yet beneath that polished surface, he never forgot the single, immutable truth of power; legitimacy alone could not protect him. Force was the bedrock of everything. And so, he built an army.

On his ranch in Texas, Vincent gathered his strength. The Corleone force was no ragtag collection of street soldiers. It was an institution. Dozens of vehicles; cars, buses and trucks stood ready. More than twenty helicopters, a handful of private jets, and a stockpile of the most advanced weaponry money could buy. He had the means to send his men anywhere, with a swiftness that dazzled even his enemies. Sicily might still matter to the Corleones in heritage and symbolism, but Vincent resolved never again to rely on it. His empire would take root solely in America, nourished by its soil and bounded by its borders; its strength drawn from the only land he trusted. Yet power carried its own cruel toll. Vincent's path had demanded sacrifices, none greater than Mary Corleone, the last and truest love of his life. Like her father before him, he was forced to sever that bond to preserve the family's legacy. And when Mary died tragically, violently, before his eyes, the weight of that choice crushed him. He had killed many men in his life, but nothing wounded him like watching her fall. He saw Michael, once the coldest, most unshakable of men shattered in grief, even after avenging her death. In that moment, something broke within Vincent too, leaving a scar that would never heal. He came to believe Mary's death was no accident, but a punishment. A message from God, harsh and undeniable, warning him of the exorbitant price of the life he had embraced. From that day forward, Vincent swore off marriage, swore off love. His heart was sealed. To him, Sicily became cursed earth, heavy with omens and eternal mourning. He resolved never to return. Don Vincent Corleone had risen higher than any Corleone before him; wily, relentless, commanding. But all his empire, all his power, stood on the bones of what he had lost. Despite the unimaginable fortune he had built, wealth for which men would fight, kill, and die, Vincent Corleone found himself denied the one treasure he longed for most: peace of mind. His empire stretched from the advertising giant in Boston to the financial institution in Chicago, from the prestigious law firm in New York to glittering hotels in Las Vegas and the Caribbean. And, beneath it all, the dark engine that fueled so much of his power; arms trafficking. Yet none of it, not the corporations, not the fortune, not the empire, could quiet the gnawing unrest that shadowed him night and day. It was peace he craved; the kind of peace that might have allowed him to live without the suffocating fear of the unknown, without the constant suspicion of what fate might be concealing, waiting to strike. Peace enough to build a family of his own, to take a wife, to raise children who would bear his name, inherit his fortune, and perpetuate the Corleone legacy. But that peace had always eluded the Corleones. It was the one inheritance no Don ever managed to secure. Vincent carried his own scars. As a child and adolescent, he had borne the humiliation of growing up without a father, enduring the pejorative sting of being branded "the bastard" by schoolmates, and later, by enemies in the underworld. He had worn that stigma like a mark on his flesh. Never, in his darkest imaginings, did he believe it would pass on to the one he would one day love the most; his own son...

Indeed, this was the life Don Vincent Corleone had chosen of his own volition. A life steeped in plots and betrayals, built on fear and bloodshed, commanded with an iron will that allowed no margin for error. Treachery and incompetence; those were the sins he despised above all others. He understood, with crystalline clarity, that they were the twin assassins of success, and he allowed neither to find purchase in his empire. And yet, for all his power, his life was stripped bare of serenity, of comfort, of guarantees, and worst of all, of love. That was the cost, the unbearable cost, he had pledged himself to pay. The discipline he had sworn never to break. Until that momentous afternoon at Denari's Restaurant. Until Claudia Soleri walked into his world...

After Robert's birth, Claudia's resolve hardened. From that moment on, certain truths became nonnegotiable. She was ever mindful of her sacred duty to her only son, fully aware that his arrival in her life was no accident. What she had once feared as a mistake, she now recognized as something closer to providence; a message hammered home by fate, if not by God Himself. Robert changed everything. He became her axis, her reason for being. Where her life had once been barren and meaningless, it now brimmed with a sense of purpose; cheerful, even, at this fragile juncture. For the first time, she had someone to live for, someone to protect. It was an intractable burden, yes, but one she embraced with fierce devotion. Before worrying about how to raise him alone, how to be both father and mother, Claudia made a few hard decisions. No one, no matter how close, and nothing, no matter how important, would be allowed to take her attention from Robert. Not a single iota of love would be stolen from him. On that foundation, her choice about Bryan Stanley was final. He would never again darken her door. She would never see him, never let him near the boy. Late one night, after nursing Robert and laying him gently in his crib, she called Sophie. Relief surged through her voice as she whispered into the phone, "I'm so fucking glad that creature is out of my life. Relieved, way more than relieved. Glad." But relief was only the beginning. Claudia knew her son's future had to be secured. He would not be deprived of the basic care every child deserves. Yet she also swore she would not repeat her father's mistake; providing but never truly being there. Robert would not grow up with absence disguised as love. Fortune, for once, tilted in her favor. Her salary carried her for the first few weeks, and when she was strong enough to return, Nicky stepped in. He understood. He had seen the challenges awaiting her; the sacrifices, the tireless effort required of a single mother. He also knew her potential. That was why he promoted her, doubling her salary and adding allowances, making her the new manager of his restaurant. Nicky had always admired Claudia's intelligence, her diligence, her discipline, her honesty, and above all, her beauty. He teased her sometimes, half in jest, "You know, kid, if I were younger and you were a little older..." But the promotion was no act of sentiment. He was no fool. He knew the job demanded vigilance, precision, and stamina. Claudia would have to balance every detail of the restaurant with the consuming work of motherhood. That was the price she had to pay to support her son.

Yet one question haunted her, day and night.

What will I tell him when he grows up and asks about his father?

Should she invent a kinder lie, say his father had died tragically in an accident or from some nameless disease? Or should she twist the truth, portray Bryan as the reckless drunkard, the drug-addled womanizer he so often was? Or should she bare it all, the dismal truth with all its dire consequences, and let Robert inherit the horror of knowing his real father?

"What am I supposed to do?" she whispered into the darkness. "What am I supposed to tell him?"

It was the question she prayed her son would never ask...

On a warm, quiet Sunday evening in March 1984, a striking couple strolled through Central Park. From the way they walked, unhurried, their bodies instinctively leaning toward one another, and from the glances they shared, passersby could be forgiven for thinking they were deeply in love. In truth, it was only their first date. She wore a plain white ruffled shirt, its crisp collar peeking neatly from beneath a stylish blue blouse. A purple skirt, faintly striped in brown, swayed about her legs with every brush of the breeze. On her feet, chic brown heels added a grace note of height, protecting her from the chill of the ground while lending her stride a stately poise. Claudia looked radiant, every detail understated yet irresistible. He, by contrast, carried himself like a prince from some forgotten European court. And though he made a deliberate effort to appear unassuming, his elegance was impossible to disguise. Dark denim trousers, a finely pressed white shirt, a cream-and-gray seersucker jacket; all tailored to fit his lean frame. Aviator sunglasses shielded the piercing effect of his eyes, though nothing could hide the aura of command about him.

"So, what do you do for a living, Mr. Corleone?" Claudia asked, her tone curious, almost guileless.

"It's Vincent," he said gently. "You don't need to call me Mr. Corleone."

"But isn't that how people usually address you? I mean, what I saw at the restaurant that day, how everyone treated you, especially those two freaks, didn't exactly make you look like an ordinary man."

Vincent's lips curved into a sardonic smile. "And how did it make me look then, Claudia?" His voice carried a trace of annoyance.

"Like *Mr. Corleone*, not Vincent. Come on... Who are you? What do you do? And why would someone like you want anything to do with someone like me? Yes, maybe I'm easy on the eyes, but there are plenty of beautiful women more suited to you. So, tell me, what are we really doing here?"

The words flew from her like an indictment, sharp and unflinching. Vincent did not bristle. Instead, he regarded her in silence, impressed. Far from absurd, her questions revealed the steel beneath her beauty. She was neither cheap nor naïve.

"You're tough," he admitted at last, a flicker of admiration in his tone. "And very forward. Let me be just as frank. You're not the kind of girl a man fools around with. You're not stupid, and you're not easy, and I like that. But understand this: I'm not the kind of man who toys with women, or uses them to feed his appetites. I don't neglect my work or my responsibilities for foolish flings. That's not who I am."

"Work? Responsibilities?" Claudia shot back playfully. "It's Sunday, for Christ's sake."

"Weekends are for employees," he replied with quiet conviction. "Men who own the business never get the luxury of rest, not even on Sundays." As he spoke, his hand brushed a stray strand of her dark hair from her face, the gesture warm, intimate.

"You still haven't answered my question," she said, narrowing her eyes, stomping her foot against the path in mock impatience. "What do you do for a living?"

"I'm a businessman," Vincent said simply. She held his gaze, unconvinced. He sighed. "All right. I own businesses in New York, Chicago, and Boston. Two hotels in Las Vegas and abroad. A few stocks here and there." Claudia's brow arched. "Impressive. Very impressive. You must be a clever businessman indeed. But tell me, do businessmen usually walk around with bodyguards?" Her glance flicked toward the two towering men shadowing them at a distance, their eyes constantly sweeping the surroundings.

Vincent chuckled. "You don't miss much, do you?"

She stayed silent, waiting.

"They open my car doors. Carry my briefcase." His tone was dry, mocking.

"Oh, is that all?" Claudia shot back, matching his cynicism. "You hire two killers to carry your briefcase?"

That finally cracked his composure. He seized her shoulders with mock severity. "Stop asking so many questions."

"Why?" she challenged, her voice lilting, childlike.

"Because there are things you're not supposed to know." He shook his head, struggling not to laugh.

"Why?" she pressed again.

"If you don't stop asking," he murmured, leaning closer, "I'll have no choice but to kiss you."

The words stunned her. Her eyes widened, her breath caught. "Can I kiss you?" he whispered.

Her lips parted but no sound emerged. And then his mouth was on hers; warm, insistent, impossibly tender. The kiss was unplanned, uncalculated, sweet as something stolen from a dream. Like the movies, only better.

When he drew back, his voice was low, coaxing. "Claudia... will you have dinner with me tonight?"

Her heart thudded. She had never been so undone, never felt a man wield such disarming power over her; save her father, once upon a time. She wanted to resist, to pause, to think. But resistance was futile. Vincent's invitation was irresistible. Moments later, he was holding open the door of a sleek black Mercedes. And with a coy smile, she slipped inside.

A few weeks later, Nicky caught sight of Claudia slipping into a plush grey sedan after work. The following morning, he cornered her. "Where were you last night, Claudia?" he asked, his tone edged with unease. Claudia's lips curled into a pout, her dark eyes narrowing in a scowl that made plain her disapproval of his blunt intrusion. "Listen, kid," Nicky began, lowering his voice with the weight of someone trying to pierce through her innocence, "I don't mean to pry... but it's quite obvious you don't have the faintest idea what you're getting yourself into." Claudia said nothing. She folded her arms, waiting, daring him, to spell out the insinuation in his tone.

"Alright then," he muttered, jaw tight, "I'll lay it out for you: stay away from Vincent Corleone."

Her reaction was not the one he hoped for. She gave a little shrug, a defiant flicker of amusement in her eyes. "Why? What's wrong with him? He's a perfect gentleman." "He's not your type," Nicky snapped. The answer sounded hollow even to his own ears, and Claudia's face told him she thought the same. She was not buying it. "Claudia," he tried again, his voice softer now, almost pleading, "this man is dangerous. Very dangerous. He's not the kind of man your parents, may God rest their souls, would have ever wanted for you." But Claudia only stared back at him, her silence sharp and unyielding. It drove him mad.

"You're just a stupid little girl!" Nicky burst out, his frustration cracking through his restraint. "You don't know who you're dealing with!"

Her voice rose, hot with anger. "Why? What's wrong with him?!"

Nicky hesitated, then drew a breath. His eyes softened, though his words struck with the force of a hammer. "Vincent Corleone is a gangster. And not just one of those bums you see lurking in alleyways at night. No, mia cara. He's the head of the most powerful mafia family in this country, perhaps even the world. He is Don Corleone. He is the Godfather."

As he spoke, Nicky placed his hands gently on her shoulders, the gesture paternal, protective. His voice, though firm, carried a strain of compassion. He was begging her to understand, to listen, to turn back before it was too late.

After Claudia returned home, she dialed Sophie's number. No answer. She tried again, this time at the office. The phone rang endlessly before the answering machine clicked on. Claudia left a terse message, her voice urgent, almost trembling: "Sophie, please... come to my place as soon as you can. It's important, too important to wait." An hour and a half later, a sharp knock rattled the door of her apartment. Claudia opened it to find Sophie standing there, her face etched with worry.

"What's up, Claudia? Is everything alright?" Sophie blurted, her voice frantic.

"Come in," Claudia said, her tone rough, almost commanding. "I need to ask you something, and I want the truth. Nothing but the truth."

"Well, that depends on the question," Sophie replied with a half-hearted attempt at humor, a waggle of her brows.

"I'm not joking, Sophia!" Claudia snapped, her nerves fraying.

"What's gotten into you?" Sophie shot back, exasperated. "You've been acting strange for weeks; no calls, no answers, nothing. I figured you were busy, but now..." She gestured at her trembling friend. "Now I need to know what the hell is going on."

Claudia hesitated, swallowing hard. She shut her eyes as though bracing for a blow. Then the words escaped in a whisper: "Sophia... have you ever heard of a man named

Vincent Corleone?"

Sophie's eyes widened. "The Godfather? Of course. But why? Is that why..."

Claudia cut her off, voice quivering. "Is he... is he really what they say he is? A bad man?" Her tone was desperate, as though praying Nicky's warning had been nothing more than bluster. Sophie's lips tightened. Her voice shifted into the cool precision of a journalist. "You know me, Claudia. I can't accuse anyone without evidence. Professionally, I can only say that Vincent Corleone is a successful, actually a very successful, businessman." She leaned closer, her words now low, off the record. "But between us? Yes. He's no saint. He's not just involved; he runs *it* all. A real mafioso, you know what I mean? The head of the family. By far the most dangerous man alive. Claudia... is this what you dragged me here for?"

Claudia's eyes glazed over. She looked as though she had slipped into a trance, her body barely anchored in the room. "What happened?" Sophie pressed, panic creeping into her voice. "Claudia, talk to me! Whatever it is, it can be fixed; we'll fix it together. Just tell me." The dam broke. "Why?" Claudia cried out, her voice cracking. "Why did he do this to me? He was so sweet. Oh, my God..." Tears streamed down her cheeks.

"Jesus Christ, Claudia, what the fuck happened?!" Sophie's words came out in a raw shout.

Claudia buried her face in her hands, sobbing. "I'm pregnant, Sophie."

Silence slammed between them. Sophie froze, staring at her friend, breath caught in her chest. Finally, her voice emerged, hoarse, uncertain. "And... who's the father, Claudia? Please, oh please don't tell me it's..."

Claudia lifted her tear-soaked face and simply nodded. Again. And again. Until Sophie no longer had to ask.

CHAPTER THREE

RELENTLESS AMBITION

It had been his dream since boyhood: to inhabit a palace in the sky. And now, Don Carmine Capaldo called home the lavish triplex penthouse at 240 Riverside Boulevard, a monument of wealth perched above the Hudson. Its soaring ceilings evoked the grandeur of old-world estates, spread across twenty rooms and more than 10,000 square feet of polished opulence. The main floor opened into a cavernous living room, modern furniture sparsely arranged so that space itself became the luxury. Black porcelain tiles gleamed beneath an expansive gray carpet that seemed to soften the very air. Walls of glass caught the afternoon light, spilling it generously into the room and framing a view of the Hudson River, where the day's last glimmers wavered on the water. Above, the third floor housed the master suite, with its marble-clad bathroom fit for royalty. Below, in the most indulgent level of all, a bar glowed, a heated pool shimmered, and rooms dedicated to billiards, massage, and cigars made the space less a home than a kingdom.

On that late June evening of 1988, twilight mercifully swept away the oppressive heat of the day. The sky cleared into a velvet dome, stars flaring over New York with rare clarity. Inside, Capaldo emerged from the pool, his silky brown robe clinging to the dampness of his flesh. Swimming was no joy; it was medicine. A fight against the creeping stiffness in his muscles, the shadow of age that disgusted him more than any rival; early senility. The very phrase made him shudder. But tonight, his exertion was fueled by anticipation. The world was holding its breath for a spectacle: Mike Tyson versus Michael Spinks, heavyweight champions colliding in Atlantic City. Millions wagered fortunes, seduced by Tyson's ferocity, his lightning fists, his aura of invincibility. Don Capaldo was among them. He had followed Tyson since his professional debut, three years earlier. From that very first knockout, he had been enthralled.

The doorbell rang.

Charlie, Capaldo's six-year-old son, skittered to the door. Standing there was a tall, lean man with a floridly wrapped box tucked under one arm.

"Uncle Virginio!" the boy cried, leaping into his arms.

Virginio De Palma swept him up, kissing his cheek with exaggerated affection. "Don't tell your father I did that," he whispered. "You know how he feels about men kissing each other."

The boy grinned, conspiratorial.

"And where is this coldhearted bastard, eh?" Virginio teased, carrying both boy and box into the living room. Capaldo sat sprawled on a sofa, hair plastered from the pool, robe knotted loosely around his broad chest. The television boomed with the pre-fight spectacle, crowd noise filling the penthouse like the roar of an arena.

"About time," he barked. "The fight's about to start."

Virginio only grinned, holding the boy on one hip and the parcel in his free hand.

"What's in the box, Uncle Virginio?" Charlie asked, his voice full of wonder.

"This?" Virginio's eyes twinkled. "This is for a very smart young man I happen to know."

"Do I know him?" the boy pressed.

"Oh yes, you know him very well. His name is Charlie Capaldo."

The boy gasped, eyes shining as Virginio lowered the box into his hands.

"Go on," Virginio urged.

Charlie tore at the paper, revealing a board game: *Battleship.*

"It's a thinking game," Virginio explained. "For clever boys like you. Play it well, and next time I'll bring you something even better: Chess."

"What's chess?" Charlie asked, eyes wide.

Virginio laughed, booming. But Capaldo cut them off, voice sharp. "Quiet, boy. The fight's starting."

The screen flared with Tyson's entrance. The crowd roared in adulation as the champion strode to the ring, eyes like steel.

"Look at that animal," Capaldo muttered, smiling. "Would you step into the ring with him, Virginio?"

Virginio raised his palms in mock surrender. "Not in a thousand years."

Charlie, enraptured, asked, "Who do you think will win, Dad?"

"Are you kidding? Tyson, of course."

"And you, Uncle Virginio?"

"I think…" Virginio said, drawing it out, "the black kid will win."

Capaldo laughed, a harsh bark. But Charlie, emboldened, shook his head. "Spinks could win. He beat Holmes. He beat Cooney. He never lost before. He might even last the distance."

Virginio arched a brow, impressed. "Sharp analysis, boy. You hear that, Carmine?"

Capaldo waved them both off. "This'll be over before it starts. Watch."

The bell rang.

Tyson exploded forward, a storm in human form. Fists blurred, pounding Spinks backward. The challenger clinched, desperate, but Tyson's elbows dug mercilessly. Seconds later, an uppercut snapped Spinks' head back. A body shot folded him. He dropped to one knee, then staggered upright, defiant. But Tyson was ruthless. A right hand detonated on Spinks' jaw. His body crumpled to the canvas, motionless. Ninety-one seconds. It was over. "Son of a bitch," Virginio whispered, staring at the screen. Capaldo only grinned, vindicated. Charlie sat stunned, speechless. The champion stood in the ring, the crowd hailing him like Caesar returned to Rome. Tyson: undisputed, *unbeatable*, a Don in his own right, indeed.

Capaldo rose, brusque once more. "That's enough for tonight. Say thank you and goodnight to your uncle. Put the gift in your room." Charlie obeyed, clutching the box to his chest. He nearly dropped it but saved it at the last second.

"Careful, boy," Virginio said gently. "Don't lose the pieces. You'll need them."

"And how am I going to use them?" the kid innocently inquired.

Capaldo cut in, tone iron. "Read the instructions. Everything you need is in the booklet. Now to bed."

Virginio winked. "Don't worry, kid. We're not going to kiss. Just business talk."

"Thank you, and good night, Uncle Virginio," said the boy, echoing his father's instruction. He kissed his father's friend on the cheek before retreating dutifully to his room, careful not to draw the *stern* man's rebuke... Capaldo's gaze followed him for a moment; his only son, the heir to everything. After the death of Charlie's mother in childbirth, Don Carmine Capaldo swore an oath; a private, solemn vow that he would do everything within his power to fill the void her absence left in his son's life. Yet he would never do so at the expense of his own authority, or the image of the father he believed he had to be. It was a fragile balance within the Capaldo household. Charlie was his only child, and after Nadia's death, the Don never remarried. He did not live enslaved to her memory either; sentimentality was not in his nature. Women came and went; usually young, often beautiful, but none ever crossed the threshold of his home. Whenever Don Capaldo yielded to desire, he ensured that his indulgences remained hidden from the world. Discretion was his armor. Affairs were conducted in rented apartments, in hotel suites, or behind the curtained rooms of his clubs. But never, under any circumstance, under the same roof where his son slept, would he allow it. The Capaldo residence was to remain inviolate, unsullied by rumor or by taint. In the Don's mind, a borderline had to be drawn between the man and the father. Between pleasure and pride. Between the sinner and the patriarch.

Don Carmine Capaldo was born in New York, in a cramped tenement that smelled of terror and ambition, but his blood belonged to Sicily. His parents, of humble stock, came from Catania, a city crouched on the eastern coast of the island, looking out toward the Ionian Sea. They had crossed the ocean in the mid-1920s, chasing America's promise, and settled in New York with little more than calloused hands and stubborn pride. They bore five children. Three never made it past the age of five; two girls and a boy carried off before their lives had even begun. Medicine, back then, was crude, and poverty was merciless. For frail young bodies, survival itself was a gamble. Carmine, one of the survivors, carried scars from the beginning. In 1947, at twelve years old, truancy put him in front of a judge, and six months in juvenile detention changed the course of his life. Six months; that was the sentence, but for him it was a death knell. The boy was brutalized there in every way a child can be; mocked, beaten, *used*... The guards were no better than the inmates. Whatever innocence had survived in him withered away. By the time he walked out, Carmine's heart had calcified. His parents never visited. His childhood had ended behind locked doors. And then came another blow. His father, already beaten down by failure, abandoned the family without a word. His mother, Ramona, was left to shoulder the wreckage; three dead children, one son scarred by confinement, and now the shame of desertion. She found work as a janitor in the subway at Chambers Street; sweeping, scrubbing, breathing filth, just enough to keep Carmine and his younger sister, Alberta, alive. For four years their lives dragged in the same gray pattern. Alberta went to school in the mornings, worked afternoons in a pet shop across the street. Carmine dropped out for good, running errands for the neighborhood's toughs. Ramona wore herself into the ground. One morning, Alberta tried to wake her for work. Ramona never opened her eyes. Hard labor and a broken spirit had done their work. After that, the bond between Carmine and Alberta cracked apart. He could never say why, and neither could she. He shut her out, treated her with a cold indifference that wounded her more deeply than blows. She wept at night, perplexed by the unfathomable absence of brotherly affinity. Once, in a fit of rage, she had screamed at him: "You just inherited your father's cruelty! Why do you insist on treating me like that?! If you hate me so much, why don't you just fuck off and leave like he did?!" Carmine said nothing. He only stared, stone-faced, then walked away. Months later, after being gone nearly a week chasing a debtor, Carmine returned to find two policemen waiting in front of his building.

"Are you Carmine Capaldo?" asked the bigger one, voice flat and hostile.

Carmine's stomach dropped. If they had *come* for him, they would have beaten him first, cuffed him, dragged him away. This was worse. The gathered neighbors, their faces knotted with pity and disdain, told him everything before the words came.

He nodded.

"While you were gone on vacation, or wherever the fuck you were, your sister Alberta was kidnapped, raped, and murdered," the officer said, voice dripping contempt. "We need you to come to the morgue to identify the body and sign some papers, if that won't take up too much of your precious time." At the morgue, Carmine saw what was left of Alberta. He signed what needed signing. He endured the accusing stares. Then he went back to the apartment and collapsed into the one rickety armchair they owned. The ceiling above was stained and crumbling. He stared at it for hours, his mind circling the same truths: He was just seventeen. His father gone, his mother dead, his sister butchered. He had no one left. No one to care for him, no one to care about. He remembered his father's bitter laments about America's false promises. He remembered the debt he still owed to Marty Armone, his neighborhood boss, for failing to collect from Joey "the Spin." That wild goose chase had kept him away six long days. Maybe, if he had been home, Alberta would still be alive. Maybe he could have saved her. Maybe he could have shown her, just once, that he did care. Instead, he sat in the silence of the Bronx, a boy with nothing left but the ugly certainty that life had no intention of giving him a fair chance.

They sat at the bar on the lower floor, the room part library, part private club; low lights, bottles that caught the glow like jewels, a cigar smoke ribboning up to the ceiling. Don Virginio De Palma lounged with the practiced indifference of a man who had seen every argument played out a hundred times. He toyed with the stem of his glass while Capaldo stared at him across the lacquered counter, face carved in stone. "So... what is it that you want, Carmine?" Virginio asked at last, the question leaving his mouth flat and casual. Capaldo's eyes narrowed. He let his stare hang a heartbeat before the words came; cold, contemptuous. "What is it that I want?" "We need to look after our investment," he said finally, tone flattening into the sermon he used when he needed to drill a point home. "Our parents came to this land with literally nothing; they spoke no English, they had no money, no maps for this country. They worked their asses off so their children wouldn't suffer the way they did. We, on the other hand, have built something of value; businesses, influence. We paid for it with sweat and blood. Now the world moves fast.

If we don't move with it, we're finished." He took a sip of wine, a sharp inhale on his cigar, and the words poured on. "Someone is imposing on us. Someone is blocking our expansion, stalling our plans. He's conspiring up there; pulling strings that will waste everything we've fought for. By now you know who I mean."

Virginio exhaled slowly, measured. "You still haven't answered me, Carmine. What do you want, exactly?"

Capaldo's voice hardened into a snarl. "Goddamn it, what the fuck do you mean, I haven't answered? You're talking in circles, Virginio. Sometimes I think my six-year-old understands me better than you." The insult landed like a slap. Virginio's face flushed. "Don't you fucking yell at me," he snapped, standing. "Don't you ever talk to me like that, Carmine, ever. I am not one of your fucking soldiers." His hands rose, warning and furious. For a moment the two men simply watched one another; predators testing the air. Then Virginio eased back. He knew the look on Capaldo's face; the animal beneath the civility, the way anger could become violence in a heartbeat.

"You heard me," Capaldo said more quietly, but no less firmly. "You heard, but you didn't listen. And that's what makes me mad."

"All right," Virginio said, surrendering to the conversation. "Tell me, then. I am all ears."

"Vincent Corleone," Capaldo said, slow as a guillotine falling.

Virginio's shoulders tightened. "What about him?" he asked, already braced.

"If we stay loyal to that fucking snake, we are finished," Capaldo snapped. "There's money in powder now; heroin coming back, cocaine everywhere. The international markets are open like the legs of a whore; Asia, Africa, the

Middle East. There is more money than we ever dreamed of. If we take it, we can buy off police and politicians, then build an army that makes us fucking untouchable. We can outflank Vincent."

Virginio reached for the brandy and drained it in one motion, setting the glass down like punctuation. "And what do you expect the other crews would do?" he asked. "Do you really think the Colombians, the Russians, the Chinese; all those will let us move product across the globe without a fight? We slice into their territory; they'll slice back. They're not gonna stand still. And that means war."

"So?" Capaldo's mouth was a hard line. "What choice do we have? Sit back and starve while that fucker grows fat? Or seize the money and secure our future?"

Virginio's hand stilled. He looked older than his years, the map of calculation in his eyes. "Carmine, listen to me, and listen carefully, please. You are asking us to make an enemy of a man who can bring the press down on us, who has leverage in the halls of power. Do you remember how we survived all these years, and how we prospered? Was it not because we kept below the radar? Vincent has reach; men, money, influence. You talk about a hundred soldiers, fine. He can get a thousand well-trained, *very* well-trained men. We buy, let's say two hundred, he buys at least two thousand. Who survives that?"

Capaldo shrugged, as if shrugging could erase the arithmetic. "We buy more. We buy better. We make alliances." "And what about the papers?" Virginio's voice rose with the weight of the practical. "You think the media will stay silent if bodies spill into the streets? They'll clamor. The FBI will roar. Politicians will posture. Our families, Carmine, your son, my daughters, they will be in the crossfire. And now I am asking: Is the money really worth that price? Is it worth risking our lives?"

Capaldo's jaw tightened, but even his anger could not find a clear retort. He knew the logic. He also felt the hunger; the old immigrant hunger for more, the fear of falling back into penury, the desire to make his line unassailable. Virginio leaned in, voice low and fierce. "I'm telling you, for the sake of all we built; our families, our children, our businesses, I say no. We don't need that extra bloody money. Not if it means we burn everything down." Capaldo stared at him. For a long moment the air between them tasted of brandy and old grievances. Finally, Capaldo's answer was a single, hard word, spoken like a verdict.

"I can't accept *no*..."

After Don Virginio De Palma departed, leaving Don Carmine Capaldo's strenuous arguments for drug trafficking scattered like ashes in the wind, Carmine lingered before the towering mirror in his study. It was a gilded relic he had purchased at auction, said to have once belonged to the Romanovs. The auctioneer had sworn that Tsar Nicholas himself had stood before it, adjusting his collar with the same self-satisfied poise. Now, Capaldo stared at his own reflection, the glass summoning ghosts of his past one by one. They marched through his mind in relentless procession; the gray squalor of his childhood, the stinking corridors of juvenile detention, the searing memory of his sister Alberta's death. Joey "the Spin," the first man he put in the ground. The night he and Virginio schemed away their tenacious boss, Martin Armone, at only twenty-one; an audacious act that had flung open the gates to power. And Nadia; his first and only wife. The woman who had sacrificed her life to give him the son he always craved. His eyes traveled across his reflection, that face scarred forever by childhood smallpox; his badge of callousness, the mark that, along with his rasping voice, made lesser men tremble. But not all men. No, there had been one man who remained unmoved. Capaldo could still feel the heat of that day at Denari's Restaurant. The Godfather, Don Vincent Corleone, had thumped the table with contemptuous authority, reminding Carmine and Virginio of the iron law against narcotics, and of who actually sat at the top of the food chain. Corleone's eyes had carried no fear, no hesitation, only the unshakable weight of power. Capaldo's mind drifted back further, to the gritty streets of the Bronx, where he had clawed his way from nothing, scrabbling for scraps, fighting for warmth, for dignity, for survival... He had beaten the odds, bent the streets to his own will, carved out an empire. He had made himself into the man he had dreamed of becoming. His son would never know the hunger or humiliation that had been his own inheritance. And yet, something gnawed at him. Someone still stood between him and the ultimate pinnacle he pined for. Someone immovable.

That someone was Don Vincent Corleone.

CHAPTER FOUR

THE APOCALYPSE

The Big Apple; its very name hums with a kind of mythic electricity. It is, without question, the heartbeat of the modern world; vast, unrelenting, and alive in every sense of the word. The most populous city in the United States, New York has, since its inception, drawn people to it as if by magnetic force. Generation after generation, travelers, dreamers, and vagabonds alike have come chasing its promise, seduced by its shimmering mirage of opportunity and endless reinvention. Many fell helplessly in love with it. They surrendered to its pulse, made it their home, and built their futures on its restless soil, believing that here, amid the chaos and the clamor, they could carve out a destiny worthy of their hopes and their children's names. Yet, a few have turned their backs, unnerved by its density of difference, its implacable diversity, its refusal to fit into any one mold. To them, New York was a mirror they could not bear to face; its multicultural mosaic too jarring, its ceaseless energy too consuming, its truth too stark. Some whispered of a "clash of civilizations," others of disillusionment, for they had glimpsed the fragile scaffolding of the so-called American Dream and found, beneath its polish, the cracks of inconsistency.

On the eastern edge of this tense city, the Atlantic kisses its shores. And there, rising from the harbor like a copper flame, stands a figure the world has come to know by heart. Forty-six meters tall, weighing over two hundred tons, she gazes outward, torch raised high, her expression both solemn and eternal. Designed by the French sculptor Frédéric Auguste Bartholdi, with the iron genius of Gustave Eiffel at her core, she was France's gift to America; dedicated on October 28, 1886, under President Grover Cleveland's watchful eye. She is Liberty, born of Libertas, the Roman goddess of freedom. In her right hand, she holds the torch that lights the way; in her left, a tablet engraved with the date *JULY IV MDCCLXXVI*, the nation's birth. At her feet, the remnants of broken chains lie quietly, a silent tribute to the abolition of slavery. She has endured tempests, wars, and the slow corrosion of time, yet still she stands; an unwavering sentinel to those arriving weary and wide-eyed, the last thing they see before stepping onto the land of promise. They called her *The Statue of Liberty*. The world called her *The Hope*. Through her, Emma Lazarus's words still echo across the tides:

Give me your tired, your poor,
Your huddled masses yearning to breathe free...

She was meant to symbolize everything America claimed to be; the light, the refuge, the dream itself. Beyond her gaze, the city unfolds in a marvel of steel and glass, its skyline clawing at the clouds. Skyscrapers pierce the heavens like monuments to ambition, their facades gleaming in the morning light. Between them stand the older buildings, the baroque cathedrals and weathered churches, the century-old brownstones that whisper of eras gone by. The streets below throb with life; vendors shouting, taxis snarling, footsteps quickening with purpose. The scent of roasted chestnuts mingles with exhaust and rain.

New York is contradiction made visible; the grandeur of its architecture wedded to the grit of its sidewalks, the solemnity of its past entwined with the fever of its present. From the marble halls of the United Nations to the nerve center of Wall Street, from the impregnable banks guarding the citadel of American finance to the powerful media engines that shape global thought, the city does not merely exist within the world; it drives it.

Amazing. Unforgiving. Unstoppable. New York is not just a city. It is a phenomenon in all respects.

Everything was going well; well enough, at least, that nobody saw *it* coming... Claudia Soleri had found her footing at Denari's Restaurant, holding her own beneath the sharp gaze of her adamant, exacting boss, Nicky Glasses. It was not easy to earn his respect, but she had come to see the job as a test; a challenge to prove that her promotion to manager was not a matter of chance, but of absolute merit. And she was proving it every day; Claudia ran Denari's with the precision of a conductor and the warmth of a hostess born for the role. She was strict without harshness, firm without arrogance. Under her hand, every order, every shift, every detail went exactly by the book. She could calm a quarrel in the kitchen with a glance, charm a dissatisfied guest with a single word. Her grace disarmed people; her integrity unsettled them. In a city where everyone had a price, Claudia Soleri was one of the rare ones who did not. Nicky might have been too proud to say it aloud, but he admired her incorruptibility. In business, he had learned that honesty was a virtue long in decline, nearly extinct among those who sought power.

But Claudia wore it naturally, like perfume she had long forgotten she had on. She also knew how to handle men. That, too, had taken years to master; the subtle art of making them feel seen without letting them see too much. She made her guests comfortable, even charmed, yet never gave a single one an inch beyond professional courtesy. It was an instinct now, a reflex of self-preservation honed by experience and necessity. And she passed that protective instinct on to her son... Robert was sixteen; bright, handsome, and healthy, with his mother's sharp mind and her quiet determination. Claudia saw in him everything she had once hoped for herself: a second chance, perhaps, to win the life that had always stayed just out of reach. She wanted more than safety for him; she wanted excellence. Ordinary education was not enough. Her son would go to college, a good one, and graduate with a degree that opened doors. It was not a farfetched dream. It was an order. Claudia was determined to shape Robert's life around the same three virtues that had defined her own: *honesty, diligence, and discipline.* She wanted him to know his worth, to respect time, to never waste an hour chasing something trivial. She had high hopes for him; hopes that burned with the same fierce light her parents once carried for her. But in her quietest moments, when the restaurant was dark and the city beyond her window hummed with sleepless energy, Claudia prayed for something simpler; that life would be gentler to her son than it had been to her.

Townsend Harris High School stood quietly in Kew Garden Hills, a modest, middle-class neighborhood in the borough of Queens. From the outside, it looked like any other public school; brick walls, flagpole, and a courtyard that filled each morning with the laughter and noise of teenagers, but its reputation reached far beyond the borders of New York. Founded in 1904 and reborn in 1984 after decades of quietude, the school carried the name of a man who once bridged worlds; Townsend Harris, a New York trader turned diplomat, the first American Consul General to Japan. His legacy was one of intellect and perseverance, and the school that bore his name seemed to inherit both. Among the city's many institutions, Townsend Harris was a rare gem; selective, demanding, and proudly ranked among the best in the nation. It was a place where bright young minds were both tested and refined, where ambition was not only welcomed but expected. And Claudia Soleri knew this very well. From the moment she noticed her son's fascination with literature and history; the way he lingered over books, the way his questions reached deeper than his years, she understood that Robert's mind was something rare. At fifteen, when most boys were chasing distractions, Robert was chasing meaning. And Claudia, who had built her life through sheer will, was determined to give him every chance she never had; Townsend Harris became her mission. She believed the school would do more than educate him; it would shape him. It would discipline his talent, enhance his words, and open the doors that hard work alone could not. Someday, she thought, it would lead him to one of the great universities of America, the kind whose names opened futures. A university that could guarantee him something priceless; a better life than hers, a kinder destiny than the one that had shadowed their family for generations. But first things first. Before Robert could dream of college, he had to earn his place at Townsend Harris. He had to become what the students there proudly called themselves a *Harrisite*.

It began as a beautiful day; one of those rare New York mornings when the air feels almost weightless, the sky a clear, impossible blue. The sun rose bright and steady over Queens, and the humidity, for once, seemed to have relented. People moved through their routines as they always did; commuters rushing for trains, shopkeepers rolling up metal shutters, children dragging backpacks along the sidewalks. Nothing in the ambience suggested that history was already stirring.

That's how Tuesday, September 11, 2001, began.

At Townsend Harris High School, Robert Soleri sat in Contemporary History. The classroom smelled faintly of chalk dust and polished floors. Mr. Ronald Anderson, the school's distinguished history teacher, stood at the front, his voice rich and commanding as he brought to life the grim figure of Joseph Stalin; the iron-fisted architect of Soviet fear. Robert listened, or tried to. History was his domain, his passion. He devoured it the way others devoured sports or gossip. Books on revolutions, empires, and dictators filled his shelves at home. He had read so far ahead in the syllabus that sometimes, when Mr. Anderson paused for effect, Robert could already anticipate the next line, the next event, the next downfall. His classmates admired him for it; even his teachers, on occasion, seemed quietly impressed. He had a habit of outpacing everyone. But that morning, something unexpected broke the rhythm... While Mr. Anderson traced the rise of Stalin from obscurity to absolute power, Robert's attention slipped. The teacher's words, normally magnetic, faded into a distant hum. Out of nowhere, an image surfaced in his mind, vivid and inexplicable; the solemn moment two years earlier, when he and his classmates had stood in the school auditorium, right hands raised, reciting the Ephebic Oath during the Founder's Day ceremony of 1999. He could still hear the echo of the pledge, ancient and dignified, hanging in the air:

I shall never bring disgrace to my city, nor shall I ever desert my comrades in the ranks; but I, both alone and with my many comrades, shall fight for the ideals and sacred things of the city.

I shall willingly pay heed to whoever renders judgment with wisdom and shall obey both the laws already established and whatever laws the people in their wisdom shall establish.

I, alone and with my comrades, shall resist anyone who destroys the laws or disobeys them.

I shall not leave my city any less but rather greater than I found it.

It was an oath he never liked, never respected, and never really believed in. To Robert, it felt like a chain disguised as principle, a pledge that demanded obedience to rules written by others; by those whom society, in its infinite self-assurance, deemed "wise." Even as a teenager, the words struck him as meaningless.

On what grounds, he would ask himself, *does society decide who is wise enough to command the rest? By what right do men, flawed and fallible, pass laws that others must obey without question? Couldn't the authorities be wrong? Couldn't the law itself be wrong?*

The questions came in waves, restless and unyielding...

And if the law is flawed, what then of the society that upholds it? Who decides the boundaries between right and wrong? And most importantly, why do we all pretend those boundaries never shift?

Most would have brushed such thoughts aside, calling them juvenile rebellion, the usual sparks of a restive mind in adolescence. But Robert was not a typical high school student. There was something older about him, something sharper; an innate proclivity for skepticism that pulsed in his blood.

He was, after all, a Corleone.

And perhaps it was no surprise that the boy who found solace in the ruthless logic of the Red Tsar, Joseph Stalin, his unlikely idol, would look upon the sanctity of civic oaths and moral codes with cold suspicion. To him, obedience was never a virtue. It was merely a form of surrender...

It began with a sudden **blast...** A heavy, concussive bang that shook the air at 8:46 a.m., rippling through the deepest core of the city. Windows trembled. Birds scattered. No one at Townsend Harris High School knew what it meant. For a few stunned seconds, the world seemed to hold its breath. Then the noise of confusion began; doors slamming, voices rising, feet hurrying down hallways. Panic spread like a fever. Ronald Anderson was midway through his lecture on Stalin when the principal, Frederick Rally, burst into the classroom. His face was pale, drawn tight with disbelief. He gripped Anderson's arm and led him a few steps aside, speaking in a low, urgent tone. The students sensed it immediately; something was wrong.

"Apparently there's been a terrorist attack," Rally whispered. "A plane hit the World Trade Center."

Anderson blinked, uncomprehending. "What the hell are you talking about, Fredrick? That can't..."

"I'm telling you what the news said. A plane slammed into the building. They don't know how bad it is yet."

Anderson's voice faltered. "So that bang..."

"Yes." The principal's voice shook, then steadied. "We need to evacuate. Calmly. No panic. But get them home. Nobody knows what is going to happen next."

Anderson hesitated. "Are you sure it's true? Maybe it's a rumor or some kind of..."

"No, it's not a fucking rumor, Ronald," Rally snapped, loud enough for the class to hear. Heads turned. A hush fell over the room.

Then, came the announcement: "Students," Rally said, his voice tight but composed, "a tragic incident has just occurred. A plane has crashed into the World Trade Center. We don't know details yet, but for your safety, we need you to leave the school immediately and go home. This is not a drill."

The room erupted in a flurry of whispers, gasps, and hurried movement. Rally's authority, calm and commanding, kept the chaos from boiling over. Within minutes, teachers guided their students into the sunlight. Robert followed, his heart hammering. The streets outside were choked with utter confusion; parents calling on cell phones that no longer connected, cars honking in gridlock, the distant wail of sirens swelling in every direction.

Then, at 9:03, another explosion split the morning.

A nearby restaurant had a television in the window. Dozens crowded around it. On the screen, live and unreal, another plane tore into the second tower. Fire bloomed outward like a flower of smoke and steel.

"Holy shit," the Greek owner shouted. "Oh my God, this must be a war!"

Screams. Curses. The girls were crying, some boys shouting nonsense just to fill the terror. Robert stood motionless, his mind blank, his skin cold.

He thought of one thing only: his mother, Claudia.

"Where are you going?" a trembling voice called. It was Judith.

"I have to check on my mom. She's at the restaurant."

"Call me when you get back, okay?"

"I will," he said, managing a faint smile. He hugged her, kissed her broad forehead, then slipped into the chaos. When Robert reached Denari's Restaurant, Claudia was standing with her staff, eyes fixed on the flickering TV behind the bar. The images were incomprehensible; flames, smoke, ash swirling against the New York skyline.

"Mom!"

She turned, saw him, and in an instant, she was in his arms, sobbing. "Oh my God, I was about to come for you. Are you okay? Are the kids...?"

"I'm fine, Mom. Everyone's fine." He wiped her tears with his thumb. "Please stop crying. You'll ruin your makeup. That face is too beautiful for tears."

She gave a small, broken laugh. "Always the charmer."

He looked around. "Where's Nicky?"

"Still at home. I told him not to come. We're closing up. Everyone should be with their families now."

He watched her give calm orders to the staff, her voice steady despite the tremor beneath it. For a fleeting moment, he admired her strength; the kind that only comes from years of surviving fear.

"Listen, Mom," he said quietly, "I just wanted to make sure you were safe. But I have to go."

"What? No, Robert, you're not..."

He hugged her again, tighter this time. "Please don't worry."

Claudia did everything a mother could; pleading, cajoling, reasoning, even shouting through her tears, to stop Robert from leaving her. But nothing she said could reach him. Nothing could make him change his mind. And when all her efforts crumbled into despair, when the weight of helplessness finally broke her spirit, she closed her eyes, not in sleep, but in surrender. "Take care of yourself, son."

By 9:54 a.m., Robert was on the Brooklyn Bridge, running with the crowd. Sirens wailed like wounded animals. Across the river, black smoke coiled upward, blotting out the blue sky. When he reached Fulton Street, the world seemed unreal. People stood frozen, staring at the towers. And then, before his mind could catch up; the South Tower collapsed. A roar like the earth breaking open. The air turned gray, thick with dust. Screams tore through the streets. People ran, stumbling, choking, clutching strangers' hands. Robert stood rooted, numb. It was as if time itself had stopped. When he finally moved, it was toward the chaos, not away from it; a sincere desire to help, to understand. A police officer intercepted him. "Get outta here, kid! You wanna be a hero? Let the firemen do their job!" He obeyed silently, retreating toward Church Street. Around him, faces were white with ash, eyes empty. Firefighters moved like ghosts through smoke, their exhaustion written across every line of their faces.

The second tower fell almost half an hour later.

Robert remained composed. He just watched, his mind suspended between disbelief and awe at the enormity of it all. In front of a modest pizzeria, an ambulance van stood with its doors flung open. A man in a white coat stepped out, shouting to the gathering crowd, his voice cracking with desperation. "We need blood! Please, anyone who can, donate!" Robert did not hesitate. Not for a split second. He pushed through the stunned bystanders and ran straight toward the van, driven by a raw instinct to *do something*. To help. To matter. Inside, the cramped space smelled faintly of antiseptic and metal. A doctor, a middle-aged man with a neat goatee and tired but kind eyes, guided Robert to the narrow cot. His movements were rapid, efficient, practiced.

"Is this your first-time donating blood?" he asked, his tone warm despite the urgency around them. There was admiration in his eyes, the kind a man reserves for the young who are braver than they realize. Robert nodded silently, his gaze fixed on the doctor's hands.

"You're asking because there's supposed to be a two-month interval between donations, and the donor must be at least sixteen, correct?" Robert said calmly, his dark eyes bright with intelligence. The doctor chuckled softly. "Something like that." He pricked Robert's finger, glanced at the results, and smiled. "Your hemoglobin is perfect, better than perfect, actually. And your blood type..." He paused. "O." He looked up, visibly relieved. "O-type can give to anyone, but can only receive from its own. In times like this, that makes you... quite literally, invaluable." He tightened a blue tourniquet around Robert's arm, and the boy winced slightly as the vein swelled beneath the pressure. Yet there was something reassuring in the doctor's composure; the smooth cadence of his voice, the clean trim of his sideburns, the quiet steadiness in his movements.

"Here," the doctor said, handing him a small rubber grip Robert frowned, uncertain.

"Squeeze it every few seconds. Keeps the blood flowing evenly," the doctor explained gently. "You'll be done in about fifteen minutes."

Robert obeyed, the motion strangely hypnotic. The world outside; the chaos, the smoke, the sirens, they all faded for a moment into eerie silence. It was just him, the needle, and the slow rhythm of life being shared. When the process ended, Robert sat up. "Is it possible to give more?" he asked earnestly. "Since my blood's compatible with all types..."

The doctor stopped, studying him for a moment. Then he smiled, weary but proud.

"What's your name, kid?"

"Robert. Robert Soleri."

"Well, Robert Soleri," the doctor said, extending his hand, "this country could use a few more men like you. Brave, decent... and selfless when it matters most." Robert shook his hand firmly.

Outside, the wail of sirens echoed through the canyons of Manhattan. His act of quiet heroism might one day save a stranger's life, but if only that stranger knew, the blood running through their veins would not be ordinary. It would be Corleone blood.

Robert came home at eleven fifteen that night, his steps heavy with exhaustion. The day's chaos clung to him like the dust that still darkened his shoes. Claudia had been waiting by the window, her heart clenched with worry. Yet, beneath her anguish, an inexplicable calm persisted; a mother's intuition that her son was safe. She knew his heart too well. His youthful recklessness, his hunger to witness history, his desperate need to *do something*; these were not born of foolishness, but of a rare, fiery courage. A courage that, tragically, reminded her of her own father, whose valor had once cost him his life. It was the first time Robert had seen his mother so broken. Her eyes were swollen and rimmed with red, her hands shivering from hours of agitated grief. The television light flickered across her pale face as she clutched the phone, speaking intermittently with her closest friend, Sophia Flamini. Their conversations drifted between disbelief and dread, between confirming each other's safety and grasping the magnitude of what the world had become. Claudia hung on to Sophia's words not merely for comfort, but for information; Sophie's job often granted her access to truths that news anchors only whispered about. She could not bring herself to chastise her son; not tonight. His reticence, his absence all day, his impossible need to run toward danger rather than away from it... None of it mattered now. All her attention was fastened on the news, and on President George W. Bush's address to the nation. The networks aired the same four-minute speech again and again, as if repetition might make it real.

"I can't believe *this imbecile* is our president," Robert muttered, his voice sharp with disgust. "And I also can't believe *you're actually listening* to him."

Claudia ignored the provocation. She sat motionless, her eyes fixed on the screen. When the president's voice finally faded, after his condolences, his promises of justice, and his worthless benediction for a "good night", she turned toward her son and said softly, "Don't forget to call Judith. She's been asking about you all day." Robert nodded, chastened. He called Judith, enduring her anxious scolding for disappearing and for leaving his mother alone in the middle of such a catastrophe. When he finally hung up, he lay on his bed, hands clasped behind his head, staring into the dark. His mind replayed the day in relentless sequence; the Contemporary History class, the detested Ephebic Oath, the thunderous explosion, the burning towers, the screaming streets. Everywhere he looked, he had seen the same haunted expressions: fear, despair, disbelief. But above all, rage. A silent, simmering rage that terrified him more than the attacks themselves. He prayed that this rage would not take root in the hearts of those who ruled his country. That it would not beget vengeance in the deserts and cities of the Middle East, where innocent lives were as fragile as dust. Yet the world already felt altered, irreversibly tilted. Every word on television, every whisper in the streets, every politician's clenched jaw told him the same truth: September 11, 2001, would not fade. It would carve itself into history as the day the world's order began to shift. In other words, the world had just changed, and Robert Soleri had changed with it.

CHAPTER FIVE

INEVITABLE REVENGE

He was hammering through his bicep curls that Monday night, March 17, 2003, at the New York Sports Club on 2527 Broadway. Outside, the air was sharp with late-winter chill, but inside, the gym buzzed under the cold white lights and metallic clatter. On the wall-mounted TV screens, George W. Bush's face filled the frame; solemn, resolute as he delivered the stern ultimatum that would send the world hurtling toward war: "Saddam Hussein and his sons must leave Iraq within 48 hours. Their refusal to do so will result in military conflict, commenced at a time of our choosing. For their own safety, all foreign nationals - including journalists and inspectors - should leave Iraq immediately..." Within moments, the rhythmic pulse of the treadmills and the thudding of barbells fell silent. Trainers, bodybuilders, even the receptionists drifted toward the screens, clustering around them in tense silence, their reflections ghosting across the dark windows, watching the president's words like a sentence being pronounced over the world. All except for two men; he and his friend alone kept lifting. He would rather die than stop the workout...

"Think there's gonna be a war?" Johnny Cali asked, setting the heavy EZ-curl bar back on the preacher bench after his childhood friend finished a final set.

"Who the fuck cares?" the friend snapped, snatching a gulp of water. "My dad's business won't be hurt by a war. Hell, he said this could open markets for weapons. When our troops get in and kick Saddam out, there'll be chaos; buyers everywhere. Businessmen like my dad will make a fortune from arms and whatever else turns up. Then, Johnny, what do you think we'll do with all that fucking money?" He smirked and moved toward the ab machine, eyes already checking his reflection.

"By the way," he added, mischief in his voice, "how's it going with that Tiffany? The one you hooked up with last week; round tits, big ass. You score yet?"

"Mind your own business," Johnny said, stung.

An awkward silence grew while the other man tightened his core. Johnny pushed it again. "Seriously, war? You really think it'll happen?"

"What, am I the fucking president now?" the friend said. "From what my dad's saying, yeah, probably. That's why he's excited."

Johnny watched him in the mirror; the friend was obsessive about his abs. "So how exactly does your dad profit if there's war?"

"The war will happen," the friend said flatly. "After that fucker Saddam falls there'll be chaos. Iraqis; Kurds, Arabs, Shia, Sunni, they'll all scramble for power. They'll need arms. And don't forget the oil; the best stuff on earth. 'There's a fortune waiting in Iraq,' my dad keeps saying."

Johnny cocked his head. "If, when the war breaks out, you ever thought about joining up? Serving the country, Charlie?"

The question landed like a grenade. "I would've," Charlie said, voice thin, "but this fucking ulcer I've had since I was fifteen keeps me out."

"Whatever, man." Johnny laughed. "Frankly, I can't picture you in uniform, taking orders. You'd shoot the sergeant the minute he opened his goddamn mouth, *Don Capaldo...*"

"Oh, fuck off," he said, brushing off the jab, as he was heading for the locker room to take a shower, leaving the TV murmuring the rest of the president's address as if it were a distant thunder rolling over everything they knew.

It had been his dream since childhood to become an army officer. He loved guns, action movies, and contact sports; boxing above all. Any chance to flaunt his physical dominance before his classmates, he seized without hesitation. Violence thrilled him, though he had never suffered any at home. With his sinewy arms, a diamond-headed arrow tattoo etched on the right bicep, a symbol of toughness and courage, his chiseled body, above-average height, clean-shaven head, and piercing navy-blue eyes, Charlie Capaldo was the embodiment of barely contained aggression. At twenty-one, he was a high school dropout with no real purpose beyond the gym and the occasional street fight. Despite his reputation as a troublemaker, Charlie was rarely alone. Friends gravitated toward him; women, even more so. Yet he never wanted commitment. The only thing that truly interested him about women, the only thing that ever held his focus, was sex; "Pussy, Ass, and Tits," or as he liked to call them, "The Holy Trinity." Charlie was, in a way, the son Don Carmine Capaldo had always dreamed of; strong and fearless. Yet the truth was that Charlie had never achieved anything meaningful in his tumultuous youth, and perhaps it was this failure that stirred his father's pity. When people complained about Charlie's temper and insolence, especially in his school years, Don Capaldo rarely reprimanded him. Even his lifelong friend, Don Virginio De Palma, once warned, "Aren't you worried you'll spoil that boy, Carmine? You've got to teach him some respect." But whenever the subject arose, Don Capaldo brushed it aside, a passivity many mistook for indifference. Some even believed he did not love his son at all; and, at times, Charlie himself wondered the same. But nothing could have been further from the truth. Don Carmine Capaldo loved his son more than *anything*... Ever since Nadia's death, he had sworn never to deprive Charlie of a single thing, especially if it could be bought. In his son, he saw the youth he had never had, a life unrestrained, free from duty or regret, and he would shield that image at any cost. He understood Charlie's anger, his violence, and his reckless defiance. He knew what it meant to grow up without a mother; to watch other boys run into their mothers' arms while he had never even uttered the word "mom." He knew that somewhere deep inside, Charlie blamed himself for her death. They never spoke of it, but Don Capaldo sensed it, felt it in every outburst and every bruise. And so, he forgave him, again and again... Even in boxing, the sport Charlie adored since childhood, he found no real success. At sixteen, he entered an amateur tournament. His raw power overwhelmed his opponent, but his temper cost him everything. When the referee tried to break a clinch, Charlie attacked him. The result: two men hospitalized, one night in jail, and his name permanently struck from the federation's roster. Don Capaldo pulled strings to spare him worse consequences, but the damage was done. Charlie never believed in education, though his father urged him at least to finish high school. Perhaps Don

Capaldo had not pushed hard enough, or perhaps he failed to make his son understand that the world had changed, that brains now mattered as much as brawn. He wanted Charlie to one day take the helm of the business, not just inherit it. But from an early age, Charlie had decided that college and careers were for fools. His father's wealth was his safety net. Power and money would always be there, waiting. And Charlie Capaldo knew it. He knew that once *his Don* was gone, the fortune left behind would make him king for the rest of his life; even if he lived to be a hundred.

Founded in 1754 by royal charter of King George II of Great Britain, long before the United States declared its independence, Columbia University stands as the oldest institution of higher learning in New York. Without exaggeration, it remains a dream destination for students from across the nation and around the world, both undergraduate and graduate alike. Nestled at 116th Street and Broadway in Manhattan, this world-renowned university has, over the centuries, become a living monument to scholarship and inquiry in all its diverse forms. The allure of this academic sanctuary lies not only in its majestic campus and stately 18th-century architecture but also in the vitality of its student body and the distinction of its faculty. From one generation to the next, Columbia's scholars and educators have diligently upheld and expanded its legacy, transforming it into a cornerstone of global learning, and, in many ways, a luminous testament to human civilization itself.

Now might I do it pat. Now he is a-praying;
And now I'll do't. And so he goes to heaven.
And so am I revenged. That would be scann'd.
A villain kills my father; and for that,
I, his sole son, do this same villain send

To heaven.
O, this is hire and salary, not revenge.
He took my father grossly, full of bread,
With all his crimes broad blown, as flush as May.
And how his audit stands who knows save heaven?
But in our circumstance and course of thought,
'Tis heavy with him. And am I then revenged,
To take him in the purging of his soul,
When he is fit and season'd for his passage?
No!
Up, sword; and know though a more horrid hent:
When he is drunk asleep, or in his rage,
Or in the incestuous pleasure of his bed;
At game, a-swearing, or about some act
That has no relish of salvation in't;
Then trip him that his heels may kick at heaven
And that his soul may be as damn'd and black
As hell, whereto it goes. My mother stays:
This physic but prolongs thy sickly days.

"These," Professor Rudy Shapiro intoned, his voice resonating through the lecture hall, "are the words that have haunted scholars for centuries." He paused, scanning the room of motionless students. "Now, why did William Shakespeare deliberately make Hamlet delay his revenge against his treacherous uncle Claudius? The man who usurped his throne, seduced his mother, and murdered his father?" He let the silence stretch, trying to provoke curiosity, or at least wakefulness. "Come on, people," he said with a half-smile. "Help me out here. I'm in desperate need of your original thoughts."

"Revenge is a dish best served cold," one student quipped, drawing laughter from the class.

"Well, Mr. Fabien," the professor said dryly, "you'll need to provide something more substantial than a proverb." The room quieted again, the air heavy with unspoken thoughts.

Then, from the back, a calm voice broke through: "Brevity is the soul of wit."

Professor Shapiro chuckled. "Ah, very clever, and doubly so, since you borrowed that from the Bard himself. I see you're rescuing your friend from embarrassment, Mr. Soleri. Perhaps, then, you'd like to give us a proper answer?"

Robert Soleri straightened in his seat. "There are two possibilities," he began. "First, Hamlet might not have been as eager for revenge as we assume. Or perhaps he was waiting for the right moment. Killing Claudius while he was praying would mean granting him divine forgiveness, sending him straight to heaven, whereas Hamlet's own father, who died unshriven, might be suffering in purgatory. Hamlet didn't want to give his uncle that mercy. He wanted him damned for good."

The class grew still. Robert continued, his voice measured and thoughtful. "The second possibility, one I'm less fond of, is that Hamlet's rage was fueled not only by betrayal, but by jealousy. His disgust for Claudius and Queen Gertrude's relationship might have masked something deeper. Many critics argue Hamlet suffered from an Oedipal fixation; an unconscious, forbidden love for his mother. Seeing Claudius at prayer might have momentarily sobered him, reminded him that committing murder would make him unforgivable in the eyes of both God and the woman he loved most."

When he finished, the room was silent again; this time from astonishment.

Professor Shapiro broke the pause with a slow nod. "I must admit, Mr. Soleri, I'm impressed; dazzled, even. You've dissected one of the most complex figures in English literature with exceptional insight. Well done." He glanced at the clock, smiled faintly, and concluded, "All right, that's enough brilliance for one day. Don't forget, next week's assignment: an essay on the significance of Act III. It'll form a vital part of your final paper. Class dismissed."

After finishing her last final exam, she treated herself to an iced latte and found a quiet spot on the neatly trimmed lawn of Columbia University's campus. Alone, she sat beneath the soft spring sunlight, waiting for him; anxiously, almost tenderly. The chirping of birds soothed her, a small reprieve after a grueling semester. She thought about how exhausting this academic year had been, and how deeply she had longed for it to finally end. Her mind drifted to her parents; their fierce insistence that she follow in her elder sister's footsteps and attend Harvard Law School. Choosing Political Science and Middle Eastern Studies had been, in every sense, an act of *dubious* defiance, raising eyebrows about her true intentions... It ran counter to her father's wishes and, indeed, to every expectation the Eisenberg household had for her. Everyone knew the real reason she chose Columbia's School of General Studies, though few dared to speak it aloud. Yet her steadfast resolve and quiet determination eventually compelled her family to respect her decision. Not even her parents, or her sister Deborah, now living in Israel with her husband, could dissuade her from the path she had chosen, or from the boy she loved. She refused to let anyone, no matter how close, interfere in her private life, least of all in matters of the heart. Still, beneath her conviction lingered a quiet awareness, a shadow she never voiced, that her relationship with him could not last. The love she felt for him was unfathomable, ineffable, and yet, in the secret corners of her soul, she knew it was destined to fade.

"So, how did the last final go, Mr. Shakespeare?" Judith asked with a warm smile, taking a slow sip of her iced latte. Robert did not answer. He simply shrugged, as if to say there was nothing more to be done.

"Come on, don't look so gloomy," she said gently. "I'm sure you did great, as always."

He stayed quiet, though her faith in him softened the heaviness in his chest.

"Oh, come on, Robert," she pressed, tilting her head. "What's with that grim face? It's not the end of the world if you got an A–, or even a B+. You're still my favorite writer." She gave him a playful wink.

"You know what really bothers me?" he said at last, his tone subdued. "Not being understood. Professor Shapiro keeps telling me to stick to class notes; stop adding my own interpretations, stop writing what I think. He says my ideas might be wrong, even misleading."

Judith looked at him thoughtfully. "And how do *you* measure success, Robert? By your GPA, or by the credit you get for your ideas?"

"Both," he replied, half-smiling. "I want both."

She laughed softly and shook her head. "Nobody gets everything in life, my dear. My father says that every time he sees how high I aim."

"But I do want everything," Robert said quietly. Then, locking eyes with her, he added, "And most of all, I want you, Judith."

His candor struck her; unexpected, disarming. For a moment she said nothing. Then, with a faint smile, she changed the subject.

"I'm throwing a small party tonight," she said. "End of freshman year, start of sophomore life. Just a few friends; Diane and her boyfriend, Lisa and Jonathan. And you're *coming...*"

"Where are your parents?" he asked.

"They're visiting my sister Deborah in Jerusalem. Won't be back until next month," she said, catching the hint behind his question. Their eyes met, and both smiled; two minds recognizing each other's thought before it was spoken. "Be there at eight-thirty sharp," she said, feigning command before giving him a playful punch on the shoulder. Then she stood, tossed the last of her latte into the bin, and walked away, leaving him staring after her.

The Eisenbergs' apartment, tucked away in Hell's Kitchen, also known as Clinton or Midtown West, sat within the bounds of 34th Street to the south, 59th to the north, Eighth Avenue to the east, and the Hudson River to the west. It was an epitome of neatness and simplicity. Though not luxurious, its immaculate order gave it a sense of warmth and comfort that immediately put visitors at ease. The apartment contained few symbols of the Jewish faith, save for a modest menorah, nine short candles in a row, resting on an antique table beneath a vintage pendulum clock. It was here that Judith and her friends had gathered for their small celebration.

Robert was late, and the delay made Judith slightly anxious. Without drawing attention, she picked up her phone and sent him a message, asking where he was. No reply came. In truth, Robert was not eager to attend. He had never been fond of Judith's friends, yet declining her invitation was simply out of the question. As he prepared to leave, his mother intercepted him by the door, her sharp eyes studying him.

"Why are you so dressed up? Where are you going?" she asked.

"I'm not *that* dressed up. It's just a shirt, Mom," he replied calmly, a faint smile tugging at his lips.

"Are you going to stay out late?" Claudia asked slyly.

"Would you be worried if I did, Mom?" he countered, concealing his irritation at her tone.

"Take care," she said softly.

"Of what exactly?" Robert asked, folding his arms across his chest, waiting for her to elaborate.

"Of falling in love," Claudia replied. "We've talked about this before, remember? Boys and girls your age often think they know what they want, but they don't. They rush in, make mistakes, big mistakes. And I don't want you to..."

"Mom, is this really the time for this conversation?" he cut in, exasperated. "It's just a party, for Christ's sake."

Claudia sighed, half-smiling at her own worry. "You're right. Don't know why I'm being such a drama queen. Go on, enjoy yourself, Robert."

She embraced him, placing a cool kiss on his cheek before he stepped out the door.

The doorbell rang at ten o'clock sharp. Judith hurried to the door, doing her best to hide her excitement from the guests inside. Standing before her was a young man who looked strikingly handsome. His dark, glossy hair was neatly combed back, and the crisp white shirt paired with black trousers and gleaming leather shoes gave him the air of a movie star.

"You're an hour and a half late, mister. You're lucky you look so handsome," Judith said warmly.

He took her delicate right hand and pressed a gentle kiss upon it.

"Ever since I watched *Titanic*, I've always wanted to do that," he said, grinning. They both laughed softly, their voices mingling with the song of a female singer playing faintly in the background:

What would you do to get to me?

What would you say to have your way?

Would you give up or try again?

If I hesitate to let you in?

Now would you be yourself or play a role?

Tell all the boys or keep it low?

If I say no would you turn away?

Or play me off or would you stay?

Oh...

"What the hell is this?" Robert asked, frowning. Judith giggled and playfully nudged him in the ribs. "Come on, don't be such a party pooper," she teased, reacting to his sharp remark about the song playing. The moment Robert stepped into the apartment, a hush fell over the room. Every head turned toward him, and for a fleeting instant, silence reigned; an unfeigned amazement spreading among them. His striking looks had clearly made an impression.

"Robert, you look *fabulous!*" Diane exclaimed. Her boyfriend merely curled his upper lip in disdain, while Lisa and Jonathan stared in quiet surprise.

"What's your drink?" Judith asked.

Robert hesitated, unused to such attention, or rather, to being the center of it. "I'll have whatever you're having," he said reservedly.

"I'm having wine, red wine. Is that okay?" Judith replied sweetly, handing him a glass and making him slightly self-conscious under the others' gaze. They raised their glasses in a collective toast to the end of the term.

"Where were you, Robert? You've got a lot of catching up to do," said Diane, smirking.

"Well, the nap I took after lunch went a bit too long, I guess," he answered shyly.

"Do you usually take naps after lunch?" she pressed.

"No, not really," he said, his voice tinged with discomfort.

"And you decided to take one *today*... Are you and Judith planning something after the party?" Diane prodded again, her tone slurred with wine. Lisa and Jonathan shot her sharp looks, silently urging her to stop. A heavy silence followed, thick enough to cut. Finally, Lisa tried to break it by talking about how grueling the academic year had been, especially the spring semester, and how much time and effort it demanded. She spoke for nearly fifteen minutes, a valiant but futile attempt to lighten the mood. Instead, the tension only deepened. Robert stayed quiet, swallowing his irritation and Diane's impertinence alike. At last, Diane's boyfriend abruptly announced that he had an important meeting early the next morning, and, given Diane's condition, they should leave. His strained tone made it clear he was trying to patch over the discomfiture she had caused. Five minutes later, Lisa and Jonathan followed suit, their polite excuses barely concealing their relief. The evening had been blighted beyond repair.

"So, since this is your first time visiting my place, what do you think of it?" Judith asked after her friends had left.

"Do you usually ask all your guests what they think of your apartment?" Robert replied with a playful grin.

"Are you Jewish?" she teased. "Because only Jews answer a question with a question. Oh yes, they do. Your mother must be Jewish; you're far too smart for an Italian, Signor Soleri."

Her flirtatious tone made him smile. Robert did not respond right away; he simply savored her compliment. Intelligence was the one thing he took pride in; more, even, than his good looks.

"Yes, I do like your apartment, Judith," he finally said, leaning in slightly. "It's... very cozy."

"It cost us a lot when we renovated it last year," Judith replied, sensing his closeness. "Especially my bedroom. I really put a lot of effort into it." She paused, her eyes glinting mischievously. "Would you like to see it?"

Robert's smile widened.

"Are you okay?" Robert asked softly, his voice trembling with tenderness.

She nodded, a faint smile curving her lips.

He brushed a hand against her cheek, still searching her eyes for reassurance. "Was I... was it good?" he asked with a nervous laugh, trying to mask his uncertainty behind playfulness.

Judith grinned, amused by his innocence. "You really want a scorecard, don't you?"

"Of course. I'm a perfectionist," he said. "Must've inherited it from my mother."

Judith chuckled. "Then she must be Jewish; you're far too meticulous."

"Even about sex?" he teased.

"Especially about sex," she shot back, smiling.

He laughed, easing back beside her. "I'm just worried you'll get too attached now that I've shown my *exceptional talent*."

"Oh, please," Judith said, rolling her eyes. "You sound just like Diane when she's had too much wine."

The mention of her friend made them both laugh. The tension between them softened into warmth.

"Well?" Robert pressed again, his grin returning. "How did I do?"

She raised an eyebrow, pretending to ponder. "Let's just say... you'll need a few more rehearsals before opening night."

He clutched his chest dramatically. "Ouch."

Judith giggled, pulling him closer. "Don't worry, Mr. Perfectionist. You've got potential." She brought her index finger to her thumb, forming a circle, raised the rest of her fingers, winked, made a sound like the cocking of a gun, and cried out, "*ZERO...*"

"So... how was it this time?" Robert asked calmly, lying next to her.

"Rougher, but more passionate," Judith replied with a relaxed tone.

"Oh, so I scored better than a zero this time," he said with a grin. She stayed silent.

"I love you, Judith," Robert said suddenly. Still, no reply.

"I really love you. More than anyone has or ever will. More than anything else in this world. More than you can possibly imagine. I love you so much. I wish I could spend the rest of my life with you. You know, sometimes this notion crosses my mind..." He hesitated, the words catching in his throat.

"Notion? What notion?" Judith asked, her interest piqued.

"No, forget it," Robert said quickly.

"No, I really want to know," she pressed.

"It's silly... absurd, even. I'm afraid it might ruin the moment."

"Let me be the judge of that. Come on, Robert, just spit it out. Don't be so damn dramatic!"

"Alright then. Sometimes I want to stand in the middle of Times Square and scream at the top of my lungs: *Judith, I love you!* Don't give me that look; I knew it would sound childish. I just didn't know how else to prove it to you," Robert said, half-embarrassed.

Judith curled up next to him, nibbling his ear and mocking his earlier cries of pleasure. "*Aaah... Judith, I love you, I love you, I love you!*"

Robert leapt on her like an eagle swooping down on its prey, pinned her wrists with one hand, and shouted playfully, "You're a mean bitch! Has anyone ever told you that? No, seriously, you are! You're a fucking cunt!"

She burst out laughing, met his gaze, and kept teasing him: "*I'm a creeeep, I'm a weirdooo... what the hell am I doing here...*"

"But I do belong here," Robert said softly, still on top of her.

"What are you doing, Robert? Proposing or something?" Judith said with mock disbelief.

"I wish I could," he murmured. "I wish I could marry you right now; give you the best life possible. You deserve that. You really do. Oh, Judith, I love you so much..." He tried to embrace her, but she pulled away, her tone turning sharp. "What's that supposed to mean? What exactly do you want, Robert?"

"What? Why do you make me sound like some sick pervert? I didn't say anything inappropriate!" he said, deflated.

"No, Robert... it's just that I've never heard you talk like this before. You're going too far," she said, trying to calm him.

"You know," he began quietly, "when I was a kid, I heard this fairy tale; I can't remember when or where. It was called *The White Princess*. She was the most beautiful girl in the whole world, lived with her father the king in a guarded castle. Her skin was white as a dove, and her golden hair reached the ground. Many men wanted to marry her, but she rejected them all out of pride. Eventually, her father grew angry and punished her; he had her hair braided and locked her in her room until she changed. But she never did. Years passed, her father died, her beauty wilted, and when she finally wanted love, it was too late. She'd lost everything." He looked at Judith. "I think you get the moral." After a pause, he went on. "You know, my mom and I used to talk a lot about stuff like this; girls, love, marriage. She's more like a friend to me. Once, when I was fourteen, we were dining in this fancy restaurant, and there was a couple dancing. The man held his woman tight and kept whispering in her ear. Everyone watched them; the men jealous of him, the women jealous of her. But for some reason, I felt something fake about it. So, did my mom. She just shook her head and said, *'That's not the man I want you to be, Robert.'* "I didn't understand her then, but there's something else she told me I'll never forget. She said, *'No matter how many relationships you go through, or even if you marry, every love will reflect your first love...'* "And I think she was right. Tonight, I finally understand what my mother meant. Ever since the first time I saw you in the hallway at school, it was Wednesday, October 6th, 1999, I 'll never ever forget that day, I knew you were the one. You might think you're ordinary, but that's what makes you super extraordinary to me. From that day, I couldn't imagine you with anyone else. And I couldn't imagine myself with anyone else either. I've always dreamed of us. I've always dreamed of living together, forever; watching movies till sunrise, brushing our teeth side by side before going to bed.

I want that life with you, Judith. I don't want anyone else. I never will. I love you."

Judith was silent for a long moment. Then she wiped away a tear and steadied her voice. "I'm sorry, Robert. I care about you, I really do, but I don't love you. Not like that."

"Like what, then? What does that mean? Are you putting me in the friend zone now? Do you just invite guys over and sleep with them for fun?" Robert snapped.

Judith did not reply. She just sat in absolute silence, contemplating her thoughts.

"I'm sorry," Robert said quickly. "I didn't mean that. Just... tell me honestly, do you trust me? If I asked you to trust me, would that be too much? I'd do anything to make this work. Please, Judith. Just give me a chance."

She sighed heavily and said nothing.

"Goddamn it, Judith! Why are you being so fucking cruel? After everything I said, after everything I feel, why?" "Robert," she said softly, "you're a great guy. You have potential. Any girl would be lucky to have you. But you're not the one for me. I don't feel you're the man I want to build a life with. I don't know how to explain it in a rational way. *It's* just the way I feel..."

"Is it because I'm not Jewish?" he asked, his voice rising.

Judith's temper flared. "No, Robert! It has nothing to do with that! I just don't love you the same way. I don't feel safe or happy with you; not deep down. I follow my instincts, and they're telling me this isn't right. I'm sorry, Robert." Then she firmly continued, trying to put an end to this messed up situation, "I need to be alone now. Please... just go. *Get out!*"

It was late. The night wrapped everything in stark, suffocating darkness. The air hung heavy and humid; sticky, almost revolting. Robert loathed that kind of weather, when breathing felt like dragging air through water. The streets looked sinister, their weak lights flickering against the stillness. Each step felt heavier than the last, as though he were moving through a bad dream. A sense of utter desolation clung to this night. It was so damn depressing. He bought a pack of cigarettes and lit one. Though he only smoked occasionally, the stale air and the acrid smoke choked him, and he crushed the cigarette after a few shallow drags. He had no desire to go home, even though he was supposed to be thrilled about the internship he had just secured at *The New York Times*; a hard-won opportunity, arranged at the last minute through his mother's old friend, Sophia Flamini, who had fought tooth and nail to get him in. He wandered aimlessly through the city until he reached Central Park. Ever since childhood, he had been warned to stay away from the park at night; his mother's tales of muggers, addicts, and lurking shadows still echoed in his mind. But he was not a child anymore, and fear seemed almost laughable compared to the turmoil inside him. What would he do at home anyway, sitting there, steeped in this gnawing frustration? He loved Judith; deeply, sincerely. Every word he had spoken to her tonight had come from the rawest part of his soul. Nothing about his feelings was false. That's what made the rejection sting so cruelly. She was not particularly beautiful; short, with a narrow frame and a hawkish nose she wore proudly as a mark of her Jewish heritage, but none of that mattered. There was something in her that eclipsed beauty itself, something he prized above all else and found so rarely in anyone, especially a woman: INTELLIGENCE. Judith Eisenberg was not just another girl he had dated for a thrill. She was *the* girl; the one he had dreamed of. And now, she had rejected him completely, tearing apart the hope he had dared to believe in. For Robert Soleri, it was the darkest night of his young life.

As Robert wandered alone through the inky vastness of Central Park, the night pressed in around him. Then suddenly, a flicker of flame cut through the darkness. Against that brief flare of a lighter, he saw the outline of a figure; a girl, standing motionless a few steps ahead. Her shape dissolved again into the gloom as quickly as it had appeared. He turned his head, half-expecting something eerie, then resumed walking.

"What the hell are you looking at?!" a voice barked from behind her.

Robert froze. He could not see who had spoken; the park was too dark, too silent. A heavy set of footsteps approached fast, and soon a hulking figure loomed close, his breath harsh, his tone menacing.

"I'm the one talking to you! What the fuck are you staring at, boy?!"

"I wasn't looking at anything," Robert replied evenly.

"The hell you weren't. You were standing right here, eyeballing us!" The man's teeth clenched; his stare was full of threat.

Robert could tell the guy was spoiling for a fight. Still, his instinct told him to keep his composure. "It's dark," he said, voice steady. "I can't even see you. I wasn't looking at anyone."

But the man stepped in closer, his voice rising. "I don't like people staring at me! And I sure as hell don't like people talking back! Nobody talks to me like that!"

"Then stop talking to me like that!" Robert shot back, his own voice flaring now. "I just told you, I wasn't looking at you!"

The man shoved him hard in the face. "You fucker... you wanna die?!"

Robert reacted on instinct; two quick punches, a jab and a right hook, just like he had seen in the movies. He did not mean to hurt the guy; he just wanted him off. But the brute barely flinched. He came back with wild force, swinging hard. Robert tried to hold his ground, but every punch sent him crashing into the wet grass. His head throbbed; his chest burned. He was not ready for this, neither physically nor mentally. The man was too strong, too fast, too vicious. The girl fell into a trance, then bolted into the night, leaving the two of them alone in the blackness. Moments later, Robert lay sprawled on the ground, bleeding, his breath ragged. The attacker gave him a brief, contemptuous glance; just to make sure he was still alive, then turned and vanished into the shadows.

It took Robert about five minutes to regain consciousness. He was submerged in a kind of agony he had never experienced before. Even without a mirror, he could feel how terrible his condition was. But the worst part was the unbearable pain radiating from his left shoulder; it jutted grotesquely from his body. He did not know what had happened. His mind barely functioned, numbed by the waves of anguish that dominated him. Gradually, he realized that his shoulder was dislocated; something he had seen once in gym class years ago, during a basketball game. A classmate had tripped, fallen, and dislocated his shoulder. Robert remembered how the P.E. teacher had amazed everyone by popping it back in place so easily and painlessly; just sliding a hand beneath the clavicle and gently guiding the bone back into the socket. With trembling hands and clenched teeth, Robert managed to do the same. Then, limping and half-dazed, he made his way to the nearest hospital. At Mount Sinai, the doctors and nurses were visibly startled by the sight of him. His swollen face, torn shirt, and uneven gait said enough; he had taken one hell of a beating. What saddened, if not outright puzzled, everyone was that the young man before them did not look like a troublemaker. He seemed like a decent, well-mannered kid who had simply been caught in something brutal. Though Robert had managed to reset his shoulder, it still hurt intensely whenever he tried to lift his arm.

"You've got a ligament tear," said the doctor with a sympathetic frown. "We'll need an MRI to confirm, but most likely you'll need surgery."

Robert bowed his head, his jaw tightening in cold anger.

"Do you have medical insurance, kid?"

"Yes," Robert replied quietly.

"Good. I'll need you to sign some papers. It's clear you didn't fall down the stairs; this was a fight. I'm not here to judge, but it's hospital policy. You should really call your parents."

"Do you think it's necessary for me to stay here?" Robert asked.

"Yes, for observation. But first we'll do a few tests; check for concussion, brain hemorrhage, or hematoma," the doctor said, placing an ice pack on Robert's bruised face. "The nurse will take you to your room. I need to make my rounds."

Despite Robert's protests, the hospital contacted his mother; standard procedure. Claudia arrived almost an hour later, breathless and terrified. The moment she saw her son, she broke down. Seeing him like that dragged her back to the darkest corner of her childhood; to her father's decline, the helplessness etched on his face, and the heavy despair that had suffocated their home. The memory came rushing back now, raw and vivid, as if roughly three decades had vanished in an instant.

Claudia wept uncontrollably.

"I'm fine, Mom," Robert murmured, trying to calm her. "What happened?! Who did this to you?!" she cried through tears.

"I'll explain later. Don't worry. The doctor said there's no concussion or internal bleeding, thank God. But I'll need an MRI on my shoulder; it's dislocated, and probably torn. He said it's a ball-and-socket joint, and the ball popped out of place. If it's not fixed surgically, it'll keep dislocating and could even damage the bone."

"Why didn't you call me the moment you got here?!" Claudia snapped. "And who did this to you? Weren't you supposed to be at Judith's?"

Robert hesitated, unsure where to begin. When he finally told her everything, Claudia fell silent; her eyes burning with rage.

"That bitch," she muttered through clenched teeth. "I warned you, Robert. I *warned* you so many times! I told you to focus on your studies and your career; not on girls! Then, *after* college, you could think about marriage or love or whatever else. But you wouldn't listen. You just wouldn't listen!"

"What are you suggesting, Mom? That this is Judith's fault? She didn't attack me!" Robert shot back, visibly agitated.

Claudia paused, restraining her fury toward the girl who had, in her mind, toyed with her son's life.

"You've never seen that animal before?" she asked coldly.

"No," Robert said, shaking his head.

"Are you sure?"

"Yes, Mom. I'm positive."

The next morning, at 10:30 a.m., another doctor entered the room. He was slightly tall, almost bald, with a thick moustache.

"Good morning. I'm Dr. McClain, the orthopedist who'll be handling your case and performing the operation," he said with a calm, professional tone. "I've reviewed your MRI results, Robert, and you'll need surgery as soon as possible. If you're ready, we can do it today."

He pulled up a chair beside the bed and continued: "You'll just need to stay one more night for observation, and you can go home tomorrow. But you *must*, and I mean *must*, wear a sling for at least six weeks. That's non-negotiable. We don't want to take any risks. The operation and recovery need to go perfectly. I'll also need to see you twice for follow-ups; once a week after surgery, and again nine weeks later. And, of course, physiotherapy is essential to restore mobility and strengthen the deltoid. You'll need several sessions to work through the stiffness."

He glanced at Robert.

"You're still a student, right? Then it's in your best interest to have the surgery now and start physiotherapy during your summer break. That way, it won't interfere with your studies," he explained gently. The doctor's clarity and confidence reassured both Robert and his mother, convincing them to go ahead with the operation that very day.

"I'm thirsty," Robert said politely. "Could I get a glass of water, please?"

Dr. McClain smiled apologetically.

"I'm afraid not, Robert. You have to fast before surgery; nothing by mouth for at least eight hours. I know it sounds absurd, but every profession has its downsides. Ours just happens to involve annoying our patients with a long list of 'don'ts' and very few 'yeses.' Occupational hazard, I'm afraid; comes with the territory," he added with a touch of humor, declining the request.

That evening, as Robert began to emerge from the general anesthesia, the haze of the drugs slowly lifted. He felt groggy, disoriented; his mind lagging behind his senses. A brief chill ran through his body; his temperature had dropped from the anesthesia, and he began to shiver violently until the nurses quickly stabilized him. When he was finally transferred from the recovery room, the post-anesthesia care unit, he found his mother, Claudia, along with Sophie and Nicky "Glasses" waiting anxiously by his bed.

"Hi, honey. How are you feeling? Are you alright?" Sophie asked gently as she leaned in to give him a warm hug.

"I'm alright," Robert mumbled with a faint grin. "But this sling is driving me crazy."

They all laughed, grateful to hear humor in his voice.

"Oh, come on, son," Nicky joked. "From what I hear, you'll only have to wear it for six weeks; then you're free."

He paused, his tone shifting slightly. "Listen Robert, there's someone coming by to ask you a few questions. Detective Clark Johnson. Don't worry, he's a friend of mine, doing me a favor."

Robert gave a quiet nod.

Three hours later, Detective Johnson arrived. Calm, composed, with a slightly dark complexion and a pair of thick glasses that covered most of his upper face, he exuded the kind of sharp presence that made everyone pay attention. The way he walked, the way he spoke; it all carried a subtle authority.

"Sorry I'm late," he said with a thin smile toward Nicky. "Busy day; full of investigations."

He pulled up a chair beside the bed.

"How are you feeling, Robert?" he asked, his tone cool and controlled.

"I'm fine," Robert replied curtly.

"Good, good... So," the detective leaned back slightly, "you wanna tell me what happened last night?"

"I was walking through Central Park late at night," Robert began, his voice even. "And some psychopath jumped me; kicked the shit out of me for no reason."

"Was he alone?" Detective Johnson asked, keeping steady eye contact, watching every flicker of expression.

"No. There was a girl with him. She ran off as soon as it started."

"Ever seen him before?"

"No."

"Were you alone?"

Robert hesitated, then nodded.

"Yes."

He lowered his head slightly, aware of how that sounded.

"Forgive me for asking," Detective Johnson continued, "but what exactly were you doing in Central Park at that hour?" His tone had sharpened; probing now.

"What do you mean, Detective?" Robert asked, a trace of irritation in his voice.

"What I mean, Robert, is that no one walks alone through Central Park in the middle of the night; not unless they're looking for trouble. It's dark, dangerous, and filled with the wrong kind of people. If this guy wanted to kill you, he could've easily done it; and no one would ever know. So, I'll ask you again: what were you doing there?"

"I wasn't doing anything wrong or illegal," Robert snapped. "I was just taking a stroll."

"A stroll," Detective Johnson repeated dryly. "I'm sorry, but I find that very hard to believe."

His tone carried no sympathy; only quiet skepticism. Claudia stiffened beside the bed, anger rising in her chest. But the detective's questions were not random; there was purpose in every word, every pause. He was testing Robert.

Robert's patience finally broke.

"Alright, Detective, even if you think my story sounds weird or unbelievable, or even if I *was* doing something wrong, does this justify what that asshole did to me?!" He turned toward Nicky. "Is *this* your guy? The one doing you a *favor*?!"

Nicky froze, taken aback. Claudia raised her hand, motioning for her son to calm down.

For the first time, Detective Johnson allowed himself a faint smile. Robert's outburst had been unguarded, genuine, and that was what the detective had been looking for.

"Are you sure you've never seen him before?" Detective Johnson asked, his tone softening.

"Yes, I'm sure; one hundred percent."

"Alright then. Can you describe him?"

Robert closed his eyes, searching his memory, trying to piece together the shadowy face of the man; that "evil son of a bitch", as he had last seen him under the flickering city lights in the distance.

"He is white. Probably in his early twenties. And he is very well built..."

"How tall is he?"

"Hmm... He is slightly taller than I am."

"Is his head shaved?"

"Yes."

"With blue eyes?"

"Yes…"

"And a tattoo shaped like an arrow on his right arm?"

"Oh, yes…"

"Charlie Capaldo," the shrewd detective said with a heavy sigh turning to Nicky "Glasses." "That kid's been a troublemaker since before puberty. No distinction at all; he picks fights with anyone. Once he assaulted a woman; her husband happened to be a hotshot lawyer. He slapped her, she fainted. When the husband threatened to press charges, Charlie's father sent goons to intimidate him; they burned his fucking car. The next day the charges disappeared."

"Is this Carmine Capaldo's son?" Nicky asked, voice low.

"Yes." Detective Johnson nodded. "Here's the situation kid: there are no witnesses to back you up. It's basically your word against his. The injuries aren't permanent, so charges won't carry much weight. And taking on the son of one of the major players in the underworld? Not exactly a wise move."

"So, you're saying that animal will get away with it, just like that?!" Claudia exploded.

The detective's face stayed composed. "Ma'am, I just laid it on the line; the decision is entirely yours. I came here simply out of courtesy for Nicky. I can't arrest Charlie Capaldo; not because he's above the law, but because your case is weak. No eyewitnesses, no hard evidence, no motive; nothing, absolutely nothing to prove it was him. He can simply claim he wasn't there. If he beats it, and most certainly he will, he could countersue for false accusations. And if the press gets wind of it, the Capaldos will come after you with libel suits and of course the other consequences you can imagine."

Claudia stared at him, dumbfounded. Sophie reached for her hand to soothe her.

Detective Johnson leaned closer and, in a lower voice, addressed Robert: "Consider this a lesson. Be grateful that it wasn't worse. Don't drag yourself and your mother into a fight with people like that. Focus on your studies. Be smart and let it go. Let it go, Robert."

"Alright, Clark, thanks for your time. I owe you one," Nicky said as he escorted the detective toward the door. Detective Johnson grinned. "So, when can my wife and I come over for that free dinner?" he asked, half-joking. "Il mio posto è il tuo posto. You and Elizabeth are welcome at any time," Nicky replied with practiced charm.

They waited another hour. Nicky and Sophie stepped outside with Claudia for a smoke and to digest the detective's cold, practical advice while Robert lay exhausted in bed. Morphine from the PCA pump dulled the pain; three surgical incisions smarted beneath the sling. As he floated between sleep and wakefulness, his mind kept returning to Judith; to their night together, to that first reckless, beautiful intimacy, and then to the man who had ruined it. A grim, private resolve steeled inside him. If the police and the courts would not protect him, he would not simply disappear. He vowed he would never forget the motherfucker who had done this. If the law failed him, he would take matters into his own hands, prepare in secret, bide his time, and then exact his inevitable revenge on his new nemesis, Charlie Capaldo.

CHAPTER SIX

RESURFACE

On a bright Sunday noon in July 2007, he stood roughly thirty-five yards from the eighteenth hole at the sumptuous Angel Park Golf Course in Las Vegas. The round had been highly competitive, yet he managed to stay ahead of the group by maintaining his scratch score. Now, the game was nearing its end. The weather was hot but blessedly dry, the air vibrant and clear; perfect, even exhilarating, for a day on the course. He had taken up the sport some twenty-five years earlier in his leisure hours and, within five years, had achieved real mastery. Yet unlike those who fell in love with golf's quiet beauty, he was never captivated by it. He learned the game for its utility, not its charm. He understood its social value among the elite; how golf, the sport of the rich and powerful, could lubricate business deals and confer prestige. It made people in his world view him differently; more refined, more formidable. At first, like most beginners, he was obsessed with distance; how far he could drive the ball. He spent numerous hours on the driving range, enthralled by the arc of each shot. But experience taught him that distance was only half the story. The true essence of golf, the heart of excellence, lay in pitching, chipping, and putting; the short game. *Drive for*

show, putt for dough. He learned that the short game could redeem even a disastrous score, much like confession cleanses a soul of sin and offers an immaculate start.

Now his ball rested in a difficult lie. A bunker loomed in front, while behind the hole shimmered a fountain pond. He needed perfect control; too soft, and the ball would fall short, too hard, and it would vanish into the water. The breeze, light but erratic, could shift at any moment. Here lay the true test of a scratch golfer; finesse balanced with force. He took his time, calculating every variable. Years of practice, countless hours refining his touch; all distilled into this moment. His two companions, whose balls already lay safely on the green, watched from a distance: Senator Douglas Smith of Texas, and Peter Bilotti, a rising Hollywood star of Italian descent; a young man he had personally helped ascend through his vast network of connections. The caddie handed him the sand wedge. He flexed his knees slightly, bent forward at the hips, and took aim. One smooth motion; then the ball lifted cleanly, defying the sudden gust that rose against him. Despite the surge of adrenaline, his body remained composed, precise, unwavering. The ball arced through the air, landed softly on the green, rolled a few feet; and dropped into the cup. A brilliant birdie. "Wow... What a wonderful touch, Mr. Corleone," exclaimed the senator, struggling to conceal his envy of the man's one-under-par finish. Peter clapped enthusiastically, his face alight with admiration. Their scores were now a mere formality; Don Vincent Corleone had decisively claimed the round. "You know, I was worried I'd beat you today, and embarrass you in front of your guest, Godfather," Peter teased playfully, leaning close to whisper in his ear. Don Corleone smiled faintly. He had known Peter since the boy's father, Philip Bilotti, had served as his trusted consigliere; a loyal, astute man whose foresight had often proved prophetic. It was Philip who had advised the new Godfather to strengthen his private army and shift the family's enterprise from narcotics to arms trafficking; a move that later proved both wise and immensely profitable. Philip was one of the few who could address Don Corleone by his first name, a privilege almost never granted. When Philip asked him to be Peter's godfather, the Don agreed without hesitation. But a week after the baptism, Philip was killed in what initially appeared to be a deliberate car crash. Only after thorough investigation did they conclude it was an unfortunate accident. Since that day, Don Corleone had vowed to protect the Bilotti family; Philip's widow, Fiorella, and his two children, Peter and Samantha, as if they were his own. "You'll never beat me in this game, no matter how hard you try," Don Corleone said, prodding Peter good-naturedly in the ribs. "I was playing golf before you were out of diapers, boy." The three men drove their carts back toward the clubhouse. Peter, ever diplomatic, sensed his cue to withdraw. He had fulfilled his role today; serving as a bridge between his Godfather and the cunning Texan senator.

"It was truly a pleasure meeting you, Senator," Peter said cordially. "Likewise, young man," replied Senator Smith. "I wasn't sure how this round would go, but it turned out to be a delightful experience. I had a great time with you gentlemen." He smiled warmly. "My daughter's a big fan of yours, Mr. Bilotti. Would you mind if the three of us took a photo together?"

Peter laughed lightly. "Of course not. I've grown used to it by now. What do you say, Uncle Vincent?"

The Godfather hesitated. He was not fond of cameras; least of all with politicians. But before he could object, the senator reassured him: "Don't worry, Mr. Corleone. It's not for the press. Just something small for my daughter. My work keeps me away from her too often, and I'd like to show her that I do occasionally meet some interesting people..." Don Corleone gave a slow nod and forced a polite smile. The senator handed his phone to Colonel Amari, the Godfather's silent shadow for the day. Amari looked askance at his boss, aware of the unwritten rule: no photographs with business associates. "It's alright, Richard," the Godfather said quietly. "Peter is my godson, and Senator Smith is our friend."

Amari snapped the photo, handed the phone back without expression.

"Well, gentlemen," Peter said brightly, "I must head back to L.A. Filming starts early tomorrow, and I need to look presentable. Director's orders."

The Godfather chuckled. "Let's hope this picture of yours turns out better than the garbage we see on TV these days."

"Hey, Uncle Vincent," Peter replied with mock indignation, "I was nominated for an Oscar last year. And I swear this next role will win me the Academy Award."

"Are you sure of that promise?" the Godfather asked with a smirk.

"Absolutely," Peter said, his tone sincere. He leaned in, embraced his Godfather, and kissed him on the cheek. "I'm grateful for everything you've done for me; and for my family."

Don Corleone gently stroked his godson's face, a rare gesture of affection. Peter then turned to shake the senator's hand, thanked him for the game, and departed, leaving the Godfather and the senator alone to finish their quiet business.

On February 25, 1991, exactly ten months prior to the collapse of the Soviet Union, the Warsaw Pact was formally declared dissolved after more than forty-five years of staunch alliance that had bound the countries of the Eastern Bloc in unfailing solidarity. Although the defense and foreign ministers of those nations publicly announced in Budapest that the weaponry would be liquidated in accordance with terms ratified by the United Nations Security Council, a vast shadow business was taking place under the table. Countries, especially those of the Third World, in collaboration with well-connected businessmen from across the globe, saw this moment as a once-in-a-lifetime opportunity. Among the most prominent to benefit from this pivotal historical event was Don Vincent Corleone. He had cleverly, and indeed resolutely, managed to keep his family away from the narcotics trade; particularly with the rise of the legendary Colombian drug lord Pablo Escobar, whose lethal product had pervasively swept across North America. Don Corleone solemnly abided by the rules established decades earlier that strictly forbade any involvement in drug trafficking. He was even willing to go to war with Don Carmine Capaldo if the latter dared take a single step into that prohibited domain. Yet Vincent had far more to contend with after he became the Godfather. The legacy, or rather, the burden, he inherited was immense, almost unbearable, and even his uncle at the outset doubted his ability to carry it. But Vincent learned to listen. He absorbed every story his late uncle Michael had told him about how these complex fraternities were once structured; about the chain of command, and most importantly, the ancient Italian code of silence and honor known as *omertà*. He learned the appalling tales of betrayal and connivance that had scarred the family's history: from Carlo, who set up his father Sonny; to Tessio, who conspired with Barzini against Michael; and finally, to Fredo, who became an everlasting scar on Michael's soul; an indelible slur upon the entire Corleone name. From these lessons, Don Vincent Corleone resolved not to repeat his predecessors' mistakes. The most consequential decision he made was to appoint only one *caporegime*, having seen how the dual structure had always bred contention beneath the façade of loyalty, just as it had after his grandfather Don Vito's death. Thus, when Al Neri passed away in 1994, the Godfather appointed Richard Amari, Neri's second cousin, as both *caporegime* and *consigliere* of the family, an unprecedented move in Sicilian Mafia history. Colonel Amari's prowess was, and remains, phenomenal in every sense of the word. A man of exceptional strength and character, he possessed an unshakable command of firearms and a brilliant grasp of military strategy. His olive complexion, sleek dark hair, imposing stature, and hard, sculpted features commanded the kind of respect most army officers only dream of. He was an extraordinary fusion of prodigious strength and strategic resourcefulness. Amari had once served as a colonel in the United States Armed Forces under General Norman Schwarzkopf during Operation Desert Storm in 1991. His career ended in disgrace, however, when he was dishonorably discharged, though not imprisoned, for his brutal interrogation of two Iraqi soldiers captured during the Battle of Khafji. That battle, named after the coastal Saudi city where it occurred, was the first major ground engagement of the Gulf War. It lasted four bloody days, from January 29 to February 1, and represented Saddam

Hussein's failed attempt to drag Coalition troops into calamitous ground combat by bombarding Saudi positions, attacking oil facilities, and firing Scud missiles at Israel. His ultimate aim had been to seize Saudi territory; and with it, Khafji's rich offshore oil fields. That, of course, had to be stopped by any means necessary. In reality, Colonel Amari was a war criminal. He had beaten and tortured those two prisoners to death before their fellow captives, decapitating them with a blunt knife, mutilating their bodies, cutting off their genitals and forcing them into their mouths, in reprisal for an ambush that destroyed an American armored vehicle and killed its crew. This heinous act outraged both Saudis and Americans alike; a grotesque reflection of ancient barbarism that ran utterly counter to the ideals the war was meant to uphold. The scandal spread like wildfire and nearly became an international crisis, threatening to sully the reputation of the United States; the nation that had led a coalition of thirty-five countries in the name of peace, freedom, justice, and democracy. A public example had to be made, and thus, after nearly three decades of service, Richard Amari was permanently stripped of his uniform. His discharge was a great loss to the U.S. military, but a substantial gain for the Corleone family. Today, Amari oversees the training of the family's soldiers on a secluded ranch in Texas, which Don Corleone purchased to accommodate the thousand men under his command. In every respect, Colonel Richard Amari was, and remains, the man the Corleone family had long sought; a modern incarnation of the fearsome Luca Brasi.

"So, what did you want to talk to me about, Mr. Corleone?" Senator Smith asked, his Southern drawl softening as they sat on the quiet terrace of the golf clubhouse, cold beers sweating on the table between them.

The senator's posture had changed; the small talk was over. Business had arrived. Don Corleone watched him for a long breath, then spoke with the calm, deliberate cadence of a man who had learned to let others reveal themselves first. "I'm concerned about my business in Iraq. I have a large stock of weapons stored here in the States since the early nineties. I believe the time has come to move them; provide the Iraqi government with what they need to fight the outlaws and insurgents that threaten to tear the country apart."

The senator's smile tightened. "You still haven't answered my question," he said, sardonic. "What do you want from me?"

Don Corleone shifted, folding his hands between his knees and leaning forward as if to remove every possible distance. "Senator, if memory serves, we agreed that when Saddam's regime fell, I would be allowed to move my stock to Iraq. Four years have passed since Saddam's downfall and my hands are still tied. I cannot ship while others can. You have stalled me with excuses. I must begin soon; the economy's turbulence foreshadows a hard recession, and storage costs are not cheap. So, let's just say, I would rather my goods not fall into the wrong hands."

Senator Smith listened with the practiced ear of a politician, parsing threats that wore the velvet of negotiation. He grinned, insolent. "You still haven't told me, Mr. Corleone; what the fuck do you want from me?"

The senator's tone sharpened, and Colonel Amari, sitting nearby, tensed, ready. Don Corleone motioned him to stay. One glance from Amari would silence the most brazen of men.

"You keep your end of the bargain," Don Corleone said simply. "You use the connections you have to get my stock to Iraq. And, of course, you will receive a suitable percentage."

Senator Smith barked a bitter laugh. "And why on earth would I help you arm possible enemies of the United States? Have you forgotten how many American soldiers were killed by lunatic terrorists? You think I'm one of your kind; coaxing me into this filthy business? I won't be party to it."

Don Corleone's voice did not rise. He spoke as if correcting a misread map. "You misunderstand me. I have no intention of arming America's enemies. I am an American citizen, after all; I love my country. I intend to sell through the most legitimate channels, precisely so those weapons will *not* fall into hostile hands. And I thought that was crystal clear right from the start."

Senator Smith leaned in, teeth bared in a sneer. "You want to rid yourself of competition; Capaldo, De Palma, and others... You want to use me to get established, then build diplomatic ties in Baghdad and take the oil. Am I right?"

"You're laying out motives on your own," Don Corleone said, a faint smile not touching his eyes. He let the senator's words hang a moment, then unrolled the map of his case with slow precision. He spoke of logistics, of safeguards, of vetted intermediaries. He was meticulous, and every carefully chosen fact was a counterweight to the senator's accusations. Senator Smith's voice rose. "Oh, am I... You think I don't know how deals are made? Do you think my position was handed to me? I won't let you, or anyone, subvert what I've built over a lifetime. If this illicit bargain leaks, it will destroy me. You'll hide behind lawyers; I'll be the one ruined."

"Then why did you agree to the deal in the first place?" Don Corleone asked, quietly.

"Things have changed," the senator snapped. "I'm not taking any chances that could smear me and make me lose my constituents' faith."

Don Corleone studied him a beat, then tilted his head. "And you think your health condition won't shake that faith?" His tone was casual, almost conversational. "Senator, what do you think would happen if news of your leukemia reached the press?"

For the first time, Senator Smith's composure cracked. He swallowed hard. The table seemed to lurch; the cool terrace air had become thin. Don Corleone's preparation had been exact; the Godfather had researched, timed, and chosen his words to land with surgical force.

"It's still at an early stage," Senator Smith managed, voice small.

"I don't gloat over your illness," the Godfather said smoothly. "I wish you a full recovery. But I am fastidious. Preparation is respect. It is how I do business; and command it." His eyes held the senator's without flinching.

"Then what do you want?" Senator Smith whispered.

"Keep the agreement," Don Corleone replied. "My family counts on you."

Senator Smith paused, then straightened. "I'll try; I can't promise you anything..."

"Try harder this time," the tenacious Godfather said, his voice calmer than the sea. "And you don't need to worry about Carmine Capaldo. *I'm gonna make him an offer he cannot refuse...*"

The words landed like a closed door. The meeting ended. The senator left the terrace with his dignity intact only in appearance; he walked away diminished, the warmth of his earlier swagger gone. Don Corleone watched him go and, as always, returned to the patience of a man who understood how power is best exercised; quietly, irreversibly.

Nothing was more fulfilling, if not actually invigorating, than achieving what he desired without showing an iota of anger, demonstrating a shred of violence, or shedding a single drop of blood. To him, reasoning with people brought a deeper satisfaction, indeed, a greater pleasure, than money, power, or even sex. The sheer act of asserting dominance through intellect and persuasion was, to Don Corleone, an exquisite aphrodisiac. This gift, an inherited talent he had refined over time, was the secret behind the dreadful ascendancy the Corleone family had maintained over all others since its founding by his grandfather. Vincent was determined to make himself the *only* Don in America. Yet, when it came to the uneasy peace, he now shared with Carmine Capaldo and Virginio De Palma, his instincts, those same instincts he had always trusted, warned him that his leverage over them would not endure forever, despite his overwhelming clout... His primary concern, for now, was preserving the legacy his grandfather had built; the same legacy he had taken command of in its darkest hour. Still, one thought pierced through all his triumphs; unlike his predecessors and rivals, he had no heir. And that truth, more than anything, grieved him to the core. For sooner or later, everything he had fought and *sacrificed* for would fade into nothing. After the death of his aunt Connie, which followed closely upon the heartbreaking loss of his uncle Michael, there was no one left. Even his cousin Anthony, broken by the horror of witnessing his sister Mary's murder, had taken his own life in 1986 at a psychiatric hospital. Vincent Corleone was the last of his kind. When the sit-down finally concluded, the Godfather reached for his mobile phone, customarily kept silent during business, and noticed a missed call from the last person he ever expected. The name on the screen read: *Claudia Soleri.*

CHAPTER SEVEN

RESPECT IS EARNED

A plastic syringe, filled with a blend of two oily substances, Primobolan and Sustanon, was being prepared for injection into the dorsogluteal muscle. He had woken up at six in the morning, as he always did since he began training at the gym. The early days had been excruciating, especially during physiotherapy. He pushed through the tedious exercises and painful stretches, both in and out of the swimming pool, to strengthen his weakened deltoid and loosen the stiffness that had gripped his injured shoulder for months. Yet it was not only his shoulder that ached. His entire being: body, mind, and soul, was tormented by the agony of that cruel experience he had endured. The pain was everywhere; it could not be confined to a single part of him. When his shoulder finally healed and he regained full, painless mobility, he threw himself into training with dogged determination, striving to transform his physique. His mother did not stand in his way, provided his pursuit did not come at the expense of his studies. For him, building a strong body was a matter of pride; for her, finishing college was a matter of life and death. Over the next four-odd years, he followed a rigorous regimen of his own design. He went to the gym early each morning before classes, returned home afterward to study, took a brief siesta, then went back to attend his self-defense sessions before finally heading to bed. His passion for physical strength was immense, yet he was ever mindful of a crucial principle: to grow, his muscles needed rest. He learned to walk the fine line between disciplined exertion and self-destructive obsession. Training every day, he realized, would only hinder his progress. Thus, he limited himself to four sessions per week, devoting the remaining days to studying, reading, and writing articles for a local magazine; a smart way to earn some extra income. The money, along with what he drew from his bank account, covered the steep costs of supplements and anabolic steroids he habitually used. Even after graduating and starting a demanding full-time job, he maintained the same regimen. His mother disapproved of his *dependence* on those harmful, indeed, lethal, substances. But she knew it was futile to dissuade him. His heart and mind were consumed by the pursuit. And after nearly four years of tireless training and grueling weightlifting, he finally achieved his grand ambition.

As for his lost love, Judith Eisenberg, he occasionally ran into her on Columbia University's campus. They rarely spoke; and when they did, their exchanges were brief and markedly formal; as though nothing had ever happened between them... They behaved like any two ordinary colleagues. Once, she casually remarked on the considerable muscle mass he had gained. He gave a faint smile and replied, "Well, it's something new for a change," before walking away. After his graduation, they never saw or spoke to each other again. He kept a low profile, much like his grandfather had after weathering a similar heartbreak. The only difference was that, unlike his grandfather, he resolved to do something about it. Building muscle and gaining weight became his top priority. Robert Soleri wanted to be strong; very strong. But he understood that strength alone meant little; any fool could throw a punch or lift a barbell. What truly mattered was how that strength could be wielded; how it could be used destructively against anyone who dared cross him. And especially, when the right time came, against that evil son of a bitch, Charlie Capaldo.

Chelsea, on Manhattan's west side, held a well-equipped gym called Fury. It was always packed; not just with members, but with fighters; men and women who refused to stand still or give in. They came to stand up for themselves, to retaliate, to overcome whatever had hurt them by learning MMA; Mixed Martial Arts. MMA is an effective hybrid of boxing, Muay Thai, Brazilian jiu-jitsu, wrestling and judo; a rule set that allows the most functional techniques from other systems and favors what actually works in a fight. It forbids groin strikes, biting, and eye-gouging, yet remains the closest regulated thing to the stark reality of a street fight. That's why Robert chose to practice it, if not actually to perfect it. He still remembers his first day in the gym. He had been bewildered by the energy; the constant, noisy thud of kicks and punches on mitts, the unrelenting intensity of the workouts. A voice cut through the din from behind: "Can I help you, chief?"

When he turned, a medium-built man with short black hair shot through with gray looked up at him with an open, friendly face. Despite being in his mid-forties, the man projected a calm Robert instantly trusted.

"I wanna learn how to fight," Robert said.

"May I ask why? Why do you wanna learn to fight?" the coach replied with a faint smile. Robert hesitated. "Are you an actor preparing for a role? Or you wanna be like Rocky to impress some girl?" the coach pressed, trying to read the kid's story. "Yeah... especially if her name was Adrian," Robert said with a wry smile. They both grinned. The coach stepped closer, looked him square in the eye, and wisely said, "People who come here just to seek revenge don't last; here or out there."

Robert let out a heavy sigh, working to hide what burned under his skin. "My main concern is to learn to defend myself. So, when someone..."

"Oh yeah, someone; there's always a **someone**, right?" the coach cut in.

"I wanna learn how to fight," Robert repeated, steady.

"And after you learn how to fight, then what?" the coach asked, expecting something reasonable.

The coach read him, his posture, his tone, the way he dodged questions, and decided Robert was not the typical fighter... Robert watched the coach's face for the effect his next words would have, then answered, "I don't just wanna be a fighter. I wanna be a killer."

Ever since Robert graduated in the fall of 2006 with a bachelor's degree in English literature and a minor in journalism, **Summa Cum Laude**, no less, a lifelong dream had finally come true for both him and, above all, his mother, Claudia. But after the celebrations faded, he had one thing and one thing only on his mind. Apart from finding a job, no, a career, that would make him financially independent, he wanted to ensure he was ready for the moment he had been preparing for over the past three years. He wanted to be one hundred and ten percent certain that he would one day achieve a crushing victory over his bitter foe. He swore that the man who had assaulted him would never get away with it. But above all, Robert had to be absolutely sure of himself; self-critical, uncompromising, relentless. Complacency, he knew, was a luxury he simply could not afford. So, he withstood every punishing drill his coach, Donald Rogers, demanded of him; stretching his body to the limits of flexibility, absorbing the heavy thuds of takedowns to master grappling, hammering the speed bag to sharpen his hands, and skipping rope until his lungs burned to build stamina and agility. Even after he began defeating every sparring partner in the gym, he still sought new challenges. No one wanted to face him anymore. He had become a knockout artist, powerful with both hands and legs, and possessed a rare ability to shift styles mid-fight, exploiting the weaknesses of his opponents. Over time, he grew adaptable, deft, fast, intrepid; and very strong... Robert Soleri had finally become the fighter, if not yet the man, he had always wanted to be. The only thing missing was revenge.

He still vividly remembers the day his rage nearly consumed him. During a sparring session, he struck his partner with violent intent, ignoring the assistant coach's repeated calls to stop. His behavior, reckless and unsportsmanlike, forced the coach to intervene. Furious, the man ordered Robert to take it out on the heavy black sandbag. Robert obeyed, unleashing a storm of kicks and punches that brought the entire gym to a halt. Everyone watched, stunned, as he pounded the bag like a madman until a thunderous voice broke through: "Knock it off, Robert! Knock it off!" Coach Rogers shouted.

Robert stopped, gasping for air, drenched in sweat.

"Step into my office. Now. Right now!"

He followed orders, shutting the door behind him.

"What the hell was that out there?" Coach Rogers barked. "Is that what we've been training you for? Look at you, burnt out already. You think you're gonna win fights like that? You look like a bum, Robert. A bum!"

Robert's lips trembled. He tried to swallow back the tears, but failed. For the first time in years, he broke down and cried.

"Listen, kid," Coach Rogers said more gently. "I know what you're going through. Everything happens for a reason."

"No, you don't!" Robert burst out. "You have no idea what happened; or what's still happening to me!"

"Then tell me," Coach Rogers said calmly. "Talk to me like a man."

Robert did not know exactly where to begin. How could he explain everything; the father he never met, the girl he loved who never loved him back, the mother who sacrificed everything for him, and the shame he felt for letting her down after that bastard had beaten him senseless for no reason at all? All those memories collided in his mind, exploding into one unbearable storm.

"Listen to me, Robert," Coach Rogers said, lowering his voice. "And listen closely, because I'll only say this once. Sit down."

Robert complied.

"Whatever you've been through, or are still going through, that's what we call life experience. You know what that is?"

"It's... the experience one gets from life," Robert sniffled.

Coach Rogers smirked. "I credited you with a little more finesse, kid." They both chuckled weakly.

"Life experience," Coach Rogers continued, "is the sum of everything that happens to you; especially the things you can't control. If everything always went your way, then what would there be to learn? Mistakes, failures, heartbreaks, losing people you love, accidents, sickness, injustice, even getting your ass kicked; these things teach you more than victory ever will. They're painful, yes, but for a reason. Pain shows us where we're weak so we can become stronger. It reminds us to cherish what, and who, we still have. It wakes us up. Smart people learn from it. They analyze every misstep, every choice, and that understanding, paired with ambition, begets *power*. But what you just did out there!" Coach Rogers shook his head. "That won't get you anywhere, not just in fights, but in life in general. Go home. Take the rest of the week off. And think, really think, about what I said."

He placed a firm hand on Robert's shoulder. "I love you, kid. And I'm saying all this because I see something in you."

What Robert learned that day, no school or university could ever teach. Coach Rogers's words, and the compassion behind them, broadened his horizons and dispelled the darkness that had haunted him for so long. Without question, it was the most memorable day of Robert Soleri's life. His coach had taught him a lesson far greater than power or technique; strength comes first and foremost from within. He learned that life's misfortunes have meaning. That every setback can be turned into an advantage. That victory, whether in a ring or in life, begins with discipline, not rage. And he realized that, if not for that dreadful night in Central Park, he would never have met the man who later turned out to be not just his mentor, but his guide, if not actually his lifeline: Donald Rogers.

When Robert arrived at the gym at 7:15 a.m., he was planning to lift weights. It was chest and biceps day. But what happened next was completely unexpected; no, actually *fucking amazing...*

The gym was packed. Every fighter was there, and at the center stood Coach Rogers, as if waiting for a surprise guest of honor. They all tried to hide their excitement behind a calm façade. Coach Rogers approached him with a faint grin. "Well, kid, you've been nagging me for over six months to find you someone new, someone really tough, to test yourself against. Even before your graduation from college, remember?" He then pointed toward the ring. A towering black figure stood there, fully geared and ready. "Meet Henry *'The Merciless'* Colin," the coach said. "Number two heavyweight contender. One hell of a fighter, trust me. Wasn't easy to get him here, he flew in from California, but we managed."

Robert froze, caught off guard. He had not come prepared to fight, let alone someone of that caliber. "Coach... what is this? I... I don't have enough cash for..."

"Forget the money," Coach Rogers interrupted. "That's on me. All I want from you is focus. Remember what I always tell you: find your opponent's weakness; and then strike with everything you've got. You're gonna win this thing."

Robert's eyes flicked toward the ring again. "You even brought a referee," he said, half impressed, half nervous.

"I wanted this to feel like a real fight," the coach replied smoothly. "And I wanted to catch you off guard; not to unnerve you, but to keep you from overthinking."

Robert smiled faintly. "I know exactly what you mean."

Coach Rogers leaned closer, his tone softening. "Remember what we talked about that *day*; life experience.

That's what I want you to gain today, more than victory. As for winning, I'm sure that'll be the easy part. And hey, if you get your ass kicked, you can skip work and take the day off," he added with a grin.

"I'm not worried," Robert said calmly. The steel in his voice made the coach smile.

Henry *'The Merciless'* Colin was on the verge of becoming the next UFC heavyweight champion. Standing 6'5" (1.98 m) and weighing 265 pounds (120 kg), his dark skin, colossal frame, and intimidating stare; topped off with a mohawk that made him look like Mr. T in *Rocky III* were enough to make most men tremble. For Robert, it was the greatest test of his life. The odds were stacked high against him, but his will to prove himself burned higher still. The atmosphere was electric. Fighters crowded around the ring, whispering, vibrating with anticipation. Some wanted to see Robert finally humbled; others rooted for him to win, proud that he represented their gym. Coach Rogers, however, watched like a man about to witness the harvest of roughly four years' labor. When the referee signaled for the fight to begin, Robert extended his fist in a gesture of respect; expecting the customary tap. To everyone's surprise, Henry ignored it and lunged forward. From the first exchange, Robert read him; Henry was relying on size and reach. He wanted to clinch, drag Robert down, and end it quickly with an armbar or guillotine. And he almost did; until Robert slipped free, twisting out of the choke in a burst of strength that ignited cheers from the crowd. Now he saw it; the opening. Henry's punches, though fast, lacked the force his monstrous build promised. Robert sidestepped a long jab to his right, dipped low, and unleashed a brutal right hook; channeling every ounce of his weight into the strike. The sound cracked through the gym like a gunshot. Henry staggered, dazed, his balance broken. Before he could recover, Robert landed a savage left kick to the ribs. Everyone heard the snap. Henry winced, curling in pain.

And now came the *perfect moment*.

Robert pivoted and drove a vicious right kick into Henry's temple. The blow dropped the giant instantly; flat on the canvas, motionless. For a moment, silence. Then the gym erupted. Nobody had imagined that Robert Soleri could floor *that* man, Henry *'The Merciless'* Colin, let alone within less than a minute. Not even the referee reacted fast enough; only Coach Rogers had believed it possible. There were no cameras rolling; Henry had insisted on that. But those who witnessed it knew they had seen something unforgettable. Robert stepped out of the ring, checked on Henry, and thanked him for the match. Then he turned toward the crowd. Fighters parted before him in reverence, as if before a deity from some forgotten age. The gym exploded in applause and cheers. They were not just celebrating a win; they were honoring a man who had turned pain into power, and vengeance into victory.

Founded by journalist and politician Henry Jarvis Raymond and former banker George Jones on September 18, 1851, *The New York Times*, also known as *"The Gray Lady"*, first established its headquarters at 113 Nassau Street. After a century and a half of restless relocations from one Manhattan neighborhood to another, the venerable newspaper finally settled into an 18-story office building at 229 West 43rd Street, where it remained from 1913 until 2007. In 2003, however, construction began on a new home, a 52-story tower rising on the east side of Eighth Avenue between 40th and 41st Streets, which would ultimately become *The Times'* definitive headquarters at a cost of $850 million. Until the completion of this gleaming skyscraper, scheduled for November 2007, all employees continued to work in the old *New York Times Building*, still world-famous in its own right.

When Robert arrived at 9 a.m. sharp, the newsroom was already alive; a beehive preparing to open the floodgates to zillions of data points and innumerable stories. A scene he never truly enjoyed. Everything had to be done on time, and with obsessive precision. It was an endless race against the clock, a professional purgatory governed by the ruthless journalistic axiom: *"If it bleeds, it leads."* Day after day, he stomached the absurd, and often gory, details of the stories he was tasked to proofread, edit, or redact. No matter how much he detested it, he had no choice. It came with the territory. Robert had loved writing ever since he was a schoolboy. But the unimaginable pressure of his daily work, nerve-racking beyond belief, had extinguished much of the passion he once had for his craft. Perhaps it was because it no longer resembled the innocent, carefree days of school and university, when he could enchant an entire class, teachers included, with his ingenuity and eloquence. Or perhaps it was because he longed for a quieter environment; one that allowed him to think, to breathe, to be himself. Or maybe, simply, he had outgrown the need for applause; he wanted something greater, something that would let him *lead* instead of *follow*. And besides, journalism, as he was taught at both school and life, is the sworn enemy of literature. What he despised most about *The Times*, though, was the anonymity. He no longer felt special; just another number among thousands of journalists and correspondents who, over time, had lost their humanity and turned into implacable machines; some taking orders, others giving them. In such a place, to be truly recognized would take a lifetime… Still, as the months passed, he learned to tolerate this exhausting existence. After all, it was Sophia Flamini, his mother's closest friend, who had used her influence to secure him a position at what was, if not *the* most prestigious newspaper in the world, certainly among the top three. Suffice it to say, *The New York Times* is the third-largest daily newspaper in the United States, and holds an unmatched record of 130 Pulitzer Prizes; more than any other publication, at least to this day. For that alone, Robert knew he should remain forever grateful; both to fate, and to "Mighty Sophie" for granting a fresh graduate such an unrepeatable opportunity, one most journalists and editors would give their teeth for. As he sat in his cubicle that morning, his mind drifted, almost rebelliously, against the newsroom's deafening buzz. He vividly recalled the job interview that had determined his future at *The New York Times*; and how he had confidently answered every question, carefully following Sophie's advice on what employers wanted to hear. Until Mr. William Durante, the Executive Editor, leaned forward and asked him a deceptively simple question:

"What do you want from life, Robert?"

A question that seemed ordinary, too ordinary, yet carried unfathomable depth, demanding an answer only a truly nimble mind could give.

What do I want from life? That's a difficult question, a very difficult one, for several reasons.

First, every individual is different. There is no single answer that fits all. And second, perhaps more importantly, not everything we desire can, or will, come true. What we were taught in school and college, that if we work hard and make an effort, we will always enjoy the fruits of our labor, is, sadly, a fallacy. Maybe that principle works when you are still a kid.

It is the law adults try to instill in children whose minds are blank canvases. But once you graduate and collide with the real world, everything, absolutely everything, changes. If only life were that simple; you reap what you sow. If that were true, no one would simply suffer. But the world is filled with gifted and hardworking people who face endless misfortunes and uncanny obstacles that keep hounding them until they are blocked from reaching their goals. Meanwhile, others, with little talent, or none at all, live in comfort and luxury, doing nothing to deserve it, while the strivers of the world work themselves to the bone just to put food on the table.

Life is not fair. Life is not easy. In fact, life is not easy at all.

Let me first try to describe what life is Mr. Durante; perhaps that will help me figure out what I really want from it. Yes, I think that is the best way to start. Life... life is too fragile. Life is too short. But it is also mean, ruthless, unforgiving, and, above all, treacherous. To be born in a good, or at least balanced, country, one free from discrimination, racism, fanaticism, or extremism, one that offers its citizens a decent and peaceful existence, rather than constant war, political turmoil, or terrorist threats; that alone is a matter of luck; absolute luck. And to be raised by loving parents, among caring siblings, and spared any form of abuse, verbal, physical, or even sexual, is an even greater stroke of fortune. Then come the next hardships. To get a quality education, you need money; a lot of it. To find a decent job, you need connections. To find a job that makes you independent is hard; to find one you actually love is even harder. You wake up early, rush through breakfast, dress in suffocating formal clothes, speed through traffic just to make it on time, then lock yourself inside a cubicle surrounded by colleagues you neither like nor respect; who most likely feel the same about you. Yet you are forced to deal with them daily and, worst of all, accommodate their foolishness... Then comes the monotony, the tedious, repetitive work dumped on you by your asshole boss. You struggle through the hours, begging the clock to move faster. And when the long, exhausting day finally comes to an end, you drag yourself home completely drained, with no energy left to live your own life... You wait impatiently for the end of the month, just to receive that meager paycheck; barely enough to survive. Promotion after promotion, allowance after allowance, you eventually realize you would need another lifetime to truly earn what you deserve. Nurturing your potential and refining your talent is hard. Becoming the best in your field is by far harder... Falling in love is hard. Getting married is harder still. Keeping a marriage alive; that is by far the hardest of all... All these elements shape one's destiny; and together they make life so goddamn hard. And I am scared. I am so scared of not having the life I have always dreamed of. I am scared of never finding the woman I've imagined all my life; the woman I've longed for since before I even understood what love was. I thought I found her once, but I was wrong; so very wrong... And now, I need her more than ever. I need her so badly; more than anyone could possibly imagine. I've always believed she would give me the reason to keep going; the strength, patience, and fortitude to withstand life's cruelty. Especially since I never met my father. She'd give me the drive to make something of myself. Yes... yes, I am sure of it. Because love is, without a doubt, the purest and most beautiful thing in the whole world. It's what I crave most in life. It's love, simply love, that I want from life, Mr. Durante.

"He's so cute, and what a body," said one girl, checking her lipstick.

"Oh, totally. And smart, too," replied another, running her fingers through her hair.

"Is he single?" the first asked.

"No idea," the second shrugged.

"Well, I want him," the first declared.

"Sorry, honey. No chance. He's mine," said the second, firm and possessive.

"What's that supposed to mean, Veronica?" snapped the first.

"It means this guy is mine, Jessica," Veronica shot back.

"No, he's not, Veronica!" Jessica retorted.

The two glared at each other, eyes blazing, on the verge of a full-blown argument, when the door suddenly opened. Natalie Shelby, better known as Nini, the assistant managing editor at *The New York Times*, and more importantly, their boss, walked in. "Hey, what's up…" she greeted, eyeing them suspiciously. Neither answered.

"Oh, you two again," Nini sighed. "Can't get enough of each other, huh? What's the beef this time?"

"Veronica's trying to steal someone from me!" Jessica snapped.

"Shut up, Jessica!" Veronica barked.

"I don't know what's gotten into you both," said Nini, rolling her eyes, "but if you're talking about the same guy I'm thinking of, I'm afraid he's already taken."

"What?! Oh, come on Nini, that's not even fair!" both girls protested at once.

"Fuck you two," Nini said flatly. "Robert's mine. End of discussion. Now get the hell out; I need to take a piss."

Jessica and Veronica stormed out of the bathroom, muttering muffled protests as the door swung shut behind them.

A spacious venue adorned with a splendid array of tables shimmered faintly beneath the dim glow of overhead lights. At its center stood an alluring stage, waiting, almost impatiently, for performers to set it ablaze. The place was called *Music Hall*, New York's latest hotspot. It was a cabaret offering musical delights drawn from every corner of the world; from tap to belly dance, hip-hop to jazz, oriental to western. Any rhythm one could imagine found its place there, as long as it carried genuine flair. He, however, was not thrilled. In truth, he was not eager to go out with her at all. But she had been flirting and pestering him for weeks, her persistence revealing a determination he almost admired; but not enough to reciprocate. He was not interested. Not in her, not in anyone. Not now. He was still wounded, and the thought of dating for distraction repelled him. He could never bring himself to indulge in such moral emptiness. Cheapening himself was not his style; nor could he bear the idea of using someone, physically or emotionally. While some men lived by the so-called "Triple F Rule"; Find them, Fuck them, Forget them, he never subscribed to it. He refused to see women as mere conquests. What he longed for was something real; the image of being with a woman he truly loved. The apple, after all, does not fall far from the tree...

When Robert and Nini entered the cabaret, took their seats at the table she had reserved, and ordered a bottle of wine, they soon found themselves, along with the rest of the audience, utterly captivated by a remarkable ensemble of guitarists. Their performance spanned a medley of songs, crowned by an unforgettable rendition of *Hotel California* that cast a spell over everyone present. As the show went on, the sumptuous food and intoxicating wine elevated the evening to pure delight.

"Are you having a good time?" Nini asked softly.

He did not answer; just offered a calm smile and a faint nod, enough for her to sense how his mood had shifted, how he had finally relaxed. She began to realize that his enjoyment had little to do with her and everything to do with the bustling, exhilarating atmosphere surrounding them. The Saturday night program at *Music Hall* featured a lineup of exceptional performers who filled the room with infectious euphoria. Laughter rippled through the crowd; couples kissed, embraced, and swayed together. No one could have foreseen, however, the profound effect the final song would have on them all... Nini could not take her eyes off Robert, who looked exceptionally handsome that night. She tried, she truly tried, to restrain the surge of desire coursing through her, but the wine and the intoxicating ambience of *Music Hall* made resistance impossible. She leaned in and kissed him, pressing her lips against his, then slipped her tongue into his lush mouth for a few lingering seconds. To her surprise, he did not pull away. On the contrary, he seemed to enjoy her boldness, or rather, her kissing skills, especially under the gaze of everyone around them.

"You're so sweet," Nini murmured tenderly.

Robert remained upright, calm and composed, his face unreadable. A moment later, she nestled her head on his left shoulder with a sense of ease, as if they had been together for years. They continued to savor the show, enchanted by the night's remarkable performers; until an unfamiliar singer, a man in his late twenties, took the stage. Accompanied by seven musicians, he introduced himself with the confidence of a seasoned star:

"Good evening, ladies and gentlemen. I'm Mark Benedetti, and these fine people beside me are my friends, who graciously agreed to play with me tonight. For that, I'm truly grateful. I wrote and composed this song, inspired by the great Greek singer Yiannis Parios, and I sincerely hope it meets your expectations. The song is called *I Cannot Live Without You.*"

That was how Mark presented himself to the audience of *Music Hall*; simple, direct, and utterly magnetic. As the house lights dimmed and only the stage remained illuminated, Mark and his band glowed beneath the beams like bright stars scattered across a night sky.

♫ ♫ ♫

All my life, I've been called a loser. I've always been rejected. My friends let me down, and even my family does not want me anymore. Nobody believes in me.

And then you happened.

The word *love* does not even begin to describe how I feel for you. But I have nothing to offer; nothing but myself. Now I have this chance, this one chance to prove that I deserve you. Will you wait for me? Will you be the one to believe in me when no one else does? Please do...

because I cannot live without you...

No matter how long I live, I will never meet anyone like you. I will work, fight, and bleed to prove I'm worthy of you; and even if I die trying, I'll die happy, knowing you deserve the best. Because I know, with every breath I take, that I cannot live without you.

I will endure the long nights of estrangement. I will withstand the agony of loneliness. I will rebuild myself from the ground up. My only comfort while I'm far from you will be knowing that you're waiting for me. The image of you in your wedding dress, smiling as if the world itself had stopped to watch you, gives me strength. That smile alone makes me willing to go through hell; because I cannot live without you.

♫ ♫ ♫

When Mark finished, the room fell silent for a few seconds, as if struck by lightning. His song, and that deep, melodious voice, left everyone stunned. Mark's set closed the night, capping a string of spectacular performances and making it one of Music Hall's most successful nights. The applause that followed was immediate and thunderous. People rose to their feet, shouting and cheering; proof of how much the crowd admired the singer's rare talent. Robert could not leave without meeting him. It took time to push through the swarm of fans, but somehow Mark noticed Robert as if they had known each other for years. Robert and Nini introduced themselves, shook hands, and exchanged numbers amid the chaos. As they threaded their way out, something stopped Robert cold: a face in the crowd that tugged at a memory; familiar in the worst way. Charlie Capaldo. The image flooded back; the shaved head, the build, the posture. A surge of anger hit him like a physical blow. *Is this him? Why here? And why now?* He felt the old rage rise. *Do I walk away? Let it go; it has been four years. Fuck no. I must take revenge. But what about Nini? Oh, fuck Nini. I will kill this motherfucker.*

He excused himself and moved closer, needing to be sure. He had to see the face, the eyes; the detail that would confirm it. At the right angle, when the features were finally clear, Robert exhaled. It was not Charlie Capaldo. It was someone else.

"Oh Jesus, Robert... that was incredible," Nini murmured breathlessly, resting her head against his chest. "You are truly blessed; your looks, your mind, your body, your dick... everything about you just feels perfect."

Robert smiled faintly, his gaze fixed on the ceiling. "I'm flattered, Nini."

She traced a finger along his arm, admiring the sculpted muscle beneath his skin. "You keep yourself in amazing shape. I like that. And you shave your body regularly, huh? Girls like it that way. I don't know. I guess I kinda like hairy men. Not very hairy, but you know... I like to see some hair on your chest; I like to fiddle with it. And all these muscles. These arms, these big fucking arms... Most women don't appreciate men who look powerful."

"You're right. Most women don't like big *arms*," Robert replied with quiet amusement.

"Well, most women don't even know what the fuck they want... Most of them are actually stupid, and don't know how to appreciate their men," she countered softly, her tone teasing yet affectionate as she gently caressed Robert's crotch. For a moment, silence filled the room except for the faint hum of the city outside. Robert turned to her and said lightly, "You have a beautiful apartment. I like your taste."

Nini smiled, brushing a strand of hair from her face. "Oh, thank you. I like it when guests show their appreciation for my taste."

"For how long have you been living by yourself here?" asked Robert.

"I've lived here alone for as long as I can remember." Nini answered, wearing a wistful smile.

"Do you enjoy it?" Robert asked.

"It has its moments," she replied. Then, after a short pause, she added with a mischievous grin, "But tell me something; why do you still live with your mother?"

"She and I are pretty close," he said simply.

Nini tilted her head, amused. "That explains why you hesitated when I suggested coming to your place. Were you worried we'd wake her up?"

Robert laughed, shaking his head. "You know, sometimes I wonder how someone like you ended up at The New York Times. Your place is in the porn industry." She laughed too, lightly swatting his arm. The tension in the air softened into a quiet warmth, the kind that lingers when two people share a fleeting connection neither of them fully understands.

Nini was attractive, witty, and sharp; undeniably captivating in her own unrestrained way. Yet beneath her charm lay a brazenness, a kind of raw defiance that seemed to embody the most unrefined form of modern feminism... Still, Robert could not deny how deeply gratifying her presence was. With her, he felt something he had not in years; the sensation of being desired, admired, even celebrated as a man. She drew him into a world of unfiltered passion, where restraint was foreign and pleasure was the only law... And yet, for all her allure, something about Nini remained hollow to him; something he could neither define nor ignore. She lacked the quiet depth he once found in Judith Eisenberg, the only woman who had ever truly reached him. Natalie Shelby, "Nini," as everyone called her, was warm, vibrant, and generous with her affection, but she was not Judith. Robert knew it, and because he knew, he guarded himself. He refused to repeat the mistake that had cost him so much before. He would not *love* her; he would not bare his soul again. What he did not anticipate, however, was that this brief, fervent affair, one that burned so fast and bright, would end as suddenly as it began, undone by the unforeseen consequences of his next decision.

Time slipped away. Once he finished the heavy stack of work on his desk, the office boy, Damien Todaro, liked by everyone for his knack with errands and his blunt honesty, approached. "Anything you need before I leave?" he asked.

Robert slid a dossier into his desk drawer without looking up. "What time is it now?"

"Six o'clock, man. The floor's finally emptying out; everyone's gone or on their way. The next shift is about to arrive." Damien sounded cheerful.

"Yeah. The New York Times never closes. Christ... today was brutal." Robert rubbed his temples.

"You need anything?" Damien repeated the question politely.

"Actually, there is one thing," he said after a beat. "It's not work-related. I need it done as soon as possible, preferably on a weekend, and above all, with absolute discretion."

Damien's smile faded into suspicion. "What is it?"

Robert surreptitiously handed him a roll of bills wrapped with a tight rubber band. Damien blinked. "What's this?"

"That's a thousand. Tell me if you need more," Robert replied, flat.

"For what, exactly?!" Damien asked, guarded despite his fondness for Robert.

Robert stood up, then met the guy's eyes. "I need you to find me both a place and a person, as soon as possible."

"Hi... how are you?" wrote *Cindy XXX* on Facebook.

"Hey... who's this?" replied *Charles Cap THE DEVESTATOR.*

"I like your nickname," she flirted. "I'm interested in getting to know you."

"LOL, same here. That's why I accepted your request. Do I know you? Your name sounds familiar," he asked.

"Hmm... technically yes," she answered. "But I doubt you'll remember. It's been a while, and you were really wasted that night at the club." She added a few teasing emojis.

"And you're still interested in knowing me?" Charles shot back, half-cynical.

"Sure, why not?" Cindy replied lightly.

"?" he wrote.

"A friend of mine knows you well," she continued. "She made me promise not to tell you her name. But she keeps saying you're a real stud. Are you?"

"Well," he answered, "you'll find out when we meet."

"Got a picture of yourself?" she asked.

"Are you blind? My profile picture's right there," he snapped.

"I meant a nude picture, you moron," she replied with a cheeky emoji.

"You're freaking nasty, you know that?" he wrote.

"Then let's see how your 'thing' can fix that nastiness," she teased.

"I'm afraid you'll choke on it when I catch you and make you my bitch," he shot back.

"Take it out, photograph it, and send it," she dared.

He did.

"Wow... it's huge," she commented. "And looks very delicious too."

"Wanna see mine?" she added, sending him several indecent pictures.

"I wanna see you in person," Charles demanded.

"And after you see me... then what?" she asked.

"I'll give you the best I've got," he replied.

"Are you gonna be rough?"

"That depends on how you want me to be. My name's Charles Capaldo, but friends call me Charlie," he said.

"Nice to meet you, Charlie. I'm Cindy; for now. When we meet, I'll tell you my surname," she teased.

"And when's that gonna be, Cindy?"

"What about Sunday? Next Sunday?"

"Yeah, sure. Sunday's perfect. Where?"

"I live in New Jersey. Problem?"

"No problem. Where in Jersey?"

"1029 Willow Avenue, Hoboken. Be there at eight sharp."

"Sure thing," Charlie confirmed.

"It's done. That prick took the bait," she said, turning to face him.

"Good job, Lucy." Damien handed her a crumpled bill. "Here, one hundred bucks. You'll get the rest when the job's finished. And you'd better be there on time, or there'll be consequences. I'll contact you later." He said it imperiously, then left her apartment.

The house Damien had found after three weeks of searching in New Jersey was quiet, almost secluded; exactly what they wanted. He had asked a friend to scout a place outside the city at a reasonable price to avoid attracting attention. The house had been chosen to give the predator as much privacy as possible. The girl arrived at seven in the evening, just as the sunlight began to fade, dressed to provoke; tight jeans that hugged her hips and a white crop top that revealed a flat, toned stomach. At 8:17 p.m. the doorbell rang. When she opened it, a solid young man in his mid-twenties stood on the doorstep; shaved head, hulking biceps. Lucy's first thought was: what a creep. She was not innocent; she had been soliciting clients since she was sixteen and had seen every kind. Some men were ugly, some smelly and fat, each with his own bizarre fantasy... But something about this one set her teeth on edge. She plastered on a smile that hid a rising panic.

"Charlie, right?" she asked, voice brittle.

"Yeah," he answered, stepping inside with the casual arrogance of someone who thought he owned the place. "You're hotter than your pictures."

His swagger made Lucy more uneasy than any of her past customers. She realized, with a cold clarity, the purpose behind the scheme; and prayed the trap would work.

"So, you gonna tell me who you are now, or after we fuck?" Charlie leered.

"What? What are you talking about?" Lucy stammered.

He grabbed her roughly by the neck and shoved her against the wall. "Your name, bitch. Last name." His voice was low and dangerous. "You like games? I know a shitload of games."

"Cindy... Cindy Lambert," she forced out, each syllable an effort. Fear spiked through her; if this man turned violent, she could be dead.

"Wanna a drink?" she managed, trying to mask terror with hospitality.

"Yeah. A beer." He smirked. "Hope I don't belch in your face."

She handed him a cold bottle, then lied: "Oh, shit. I forgot something in the car. Give me a minute." She moved toward the door.

"No," Charlie snapped, seizing her arm. "You ain't going anywhere unless I say so."

"Let go! You're hurting me!" she screamed.

Before the scene could escalate further, a bulky figure in a red cap thudded out of the bedroom. "Let go of her, you asshole," he demanded in a voice that brooked no argument. He motioned for Lucy to get out of the apartment immediately; the girl just ran away.

Charlie charged, furious. "Who the fuck are you?" he snarled.

The newcomer did not flinch. "Who the fuck am I? I'm an old debt," he replied. "And I brought you here to pay it."

Charlie's bravado flickered. The man in the red cap was slightly shorter but heavier and far more muscular; almost double his size. Charlie's fighting experience had let him overcome bigger men before, but this was different...

"You made it easy to forget me," the stranger said, his voice thin with contempt. "Harder for me to forget what you did."

"I don't know what the fuck you're talking about boy. But you sure as hell just made the biggest mistake of your life," Charlie growled; then attacked.

The red-capped man stayed calm. He dodged Charlie's opening flurry then countered with a brutal right elbow that split the skin beneath Charlie's left eye, followed by a left hook that rattled his jaw. Charlie staggered. He tried to fight back, but the other man seized his head and drove a knee into his face, then flipped him to the floor. Charlie hit the ground hard; something he had never felt before; helplessness. The man on top of him unleashed a steady, merciless barrage of punches until Charlie's face was a mask of blood, but beneath the crimson ruin lay confusion, pure and blinding, that dominated the moment; he had absolutely no idea what all this was about. Through the blows, the stranger's voice was iron. "You beat me up in Central Park four years ago. You fucked up my shoulder. I had surgery. You humiliated me. Now you pay the price. Nobody does that to me. You hear me motherfucker. *NOBODY..*"

When the assault finally stopped, Charlie lay motionless in a spreading pool of blood. Robert Soleri, the man in the red cap, rose, breathing hard, his knuckles raw from the strikes he had landed. Robert hurriedly wiped every surface he had touched, especially doorknobs, with a handkerchief before stepping out of the house that had just been turned into a crime scene.

"Wake up, Robert! Wake up!" Claudia yelled, panic raw in her voice.

Robert stirred, still groggy. "What's wrong, Mom?" he asked, sitting up.

"Wake up!" she snapped, louder this time.

"What the hell is the matter with you, Mom?" he shot back, irritated.

"Where were you yesterday?" she demanded, cutting him off before he could answer. "And don't lie to me; don't you fucking lie to me, Robert!" Her voice shook with fury.

"I don't know what you want me to say, Mom," he said, trying to keep calm.

"I want the truth, Robert. The whole truth," she replied, hard as iron.

"I went to the gym, then I hung out with a few friends I hadn't seen in a while," he answered, forcing an even tone.

"Oh, really?" Claudia's hand closed around his wrists and she turned his palms up. "Then what are these bruises on your hands?"

Robert opened his mouth, then swallowed; words failed him. His throat worked.

"It's all over the news, Robert. Everyone's talking about Charlie Capaldo's death. I'll ask you one last time: do you have anything to do with it?" Claudia's voice was flat, deadly serious.

He hesitated, searching for a way to lie that might spare them both. "Mom, you always taught me to tell the truth," he began. "You raised me on that. I respect that, and I would never let you down, so I... I am afraid I don't have an answer to your question."

Silence pressed in on them, thick and heavy, until it shattered with a sharp slap across Robert's unshaven cheek.

Claudia's restraint broke. It was the first time she had ever struck her son.

"You asshole!" she screamed, backing away as if repelled by him. "You thought I wouldn't know? I knew it from yesterday. I knew you did something evil and despicable, because I know you, Robert. I know you, and I fucking hate you. I wish you'd been the one who died that night. Yes, I'd rather see you dead than live through this... You didn't just ruin your life. You ruined mine too. You destroyed everything I worked for, more than twenty fucking years, you ungrateful pig! You threw away every sacrifice I made so you could have a better future. Damn you! Goddamn you, Robert! You broke my heart. You broke my heart."

She collapsed into sobs, the room filling with the sound of her grief.

Robert took the day off and wandered the city, trying to find a way to claw himself and his poor mother out of the mess he had dragged them into. It was the first time he had ever seen her so furious and so broken; the image of her rage and grief gnawed at him. He hated himself for dragging her into this nightmare and spent the day turning over his next move, over and over, looking for any way to make it right.

What will happen to my mother if, no, when I get caught? Will she be able to live a normal life once everyone knows her only son, the one she sacrificed everything for, is behind bars among the worst of humanity? What a shame. What a waste. Did I mean to kill him? That's not gonna make a fucking bit of difference to the law; what happened happened. But did I really intend to kill Charlie Capaldo? No, absolutely not. If killing had been my intention, I wouldn't have spent years training; I would have simply bought a gun and finished it quickly. I only wanted to beat him badly. Somehow it spiraled out of control...

Am I happy that he's dead? "Happy" is not the word. Maybe "satisfied," or better, "relieved." Yeah, I'm relieved that I finally avenged what was done to me that night. Did I use excessive violence? He was strong; I felt I had no choice but to go hard. Was it legal or moral to unleash that force on another human being? Should I have shown mercy? Well, would he have shown me any mercy if the situation were somehow reversed? Where was his mercy that night? Where was the law then, when I lay in the hospital? Where was that detective who didn't lift a finger? And what would have happened to that girl if I hadn't shown up? Even if she is a prostitute, no one has the right to treat another person like that. If time could rewind, would I do it again? Yes, absolutely. No regrets. No pity. He was not decent. He was not even innocent. But now I must stop obsessing over this Charlie and face the consequences. I don't have a plan, and even the best plan can fail; no one truly gets away with murder, or rather, manslaughter. Still, I must leave the house tonight and find somewhere to hide. It doesn't really matter where or how. What matters the most is shielding my mother and taking full responsibility myself. I will bear the fallout alone, the crime, the mess, the stupidity, or whatever the fuck is it. This ends with me.

When Robert came home late that night, he found his mother in the kitchen; smoking. Something he had never seen her do. Her face was oddly calm, not at all like the woman who had raged hours earlier.

"I came back to apologize," he said, voice raw. "I'm sorry for the pain I caused you. No matter what happens, I'll always be grateful for everything you did for me. I couldn't have achieved anything without you. I'm going to leave now and disappear from your life. But before I go, I just wanna let you know that you are the best person I've ever known. I love you. Please forgive me."

He stepped forward to kiss her and embrace her for what he knew would be the last time, when a silhouette cut across the doorway and a voice said, brisk and authoritative, "Hurry up and pack your bags, kid. We're leaving."

Robert turned. A middle-aged man stood behind him; immaculate, quietly powerful, dressed as if for a boardroom. His very presence demanded full deference. Robert was stunned. Though he had never seen the man before, a strange familiarity tugged at him. The resemblance, or whatever it was, sent a cold, inexplicable feeling through his chest.

"Who is 'we'? And where are we going?" Robert asked his mother.

Claudia inhaled, then answered, "This is Mr. Vincent Corleone. He offered to help us in this time of trouble."

"With all due respect to Mr. Corleone," Robert snapped, "we don't usually accept help from strangers; not like this."

Vincent smirked, indifferent to Robert's protest. "I'll wait in the car. Hurry up," he said to Claudia and left.

Robert watched until the man was gone, then turned on his mother. "Who is this man, Mom? What makes you think he can help us?"

Claudia hesitated. Her silence only inflamed him. "It's quite obvious I'm not the only one keeping secrets here," Robert said, voice sharpened. "So, I'm asking again, who is he? Why is he here now? I have *this* feeling, but I need you to tell me."

Still she said nothing.

"Goddamn it, Mom, who the fuck is this man? If you don't tell me right away, I'm leaving. And I swear, you'll never see me again." He spoke louder than he ever had before. He had always respected his mother; never in his life had he shown her such fury. But at this momentous juncture, Robert *Soleri* needed the truth more than ever.

Claudia finally looked him in the eye. "Vincent Corleone is your father, Robert."

CHAPTER EIGHT

UNITY IS STRENGTH

A swarm of police cars surrounded 240 Riverside Boulevard, the residence of Don Carmine Capaldo and his late, more precisely, murdered, son, Charlie. The area teemed with armed bodyguards licensed to carry firearms, all under the direct command of their Don. Detectives and FBI agents came and went day and night, immersed in exhaustive interrogations as they struggled to unravel the brutal killing of the son of one of the most powerful Mafia figures; not only on the East Coast, but across America. Their top priority was to prevent any outbreak of vigilante bloodshed. To the authorities, Charlie Capaldo was no real mafioso. He had never been directly involved in his father's criminal enterprises. On the contrary, he was a pampered young man who understood little about the underworld and had never worked a day in his life. He lived entirely off his father's generous monthly allowances and the sizable balance in his bank account; his only source of income. His criminal record was technically clean, though he had spent a few nights in jail before his father's influence secured his release. Charlie posed no serious threat to society, unlike his father, yet he was widely deemed to be a first-class troublemaker. That contradiction left both the public and the authorities in a state of utter bewilderment. The medical report Don Capaldo received from the Office of the Chief Medical Examiner of New York City confirmed that the cause of death was a massive intracranial hemorrhage resulting from a savage fistfight. Moreover, the thorough examination of both the body and the crime scene indicated that the victim had not been outnumbered; it had been a man-to-man brawl. And since Charlie Capaldo was well-built, the police and FBI alike concluded that the assailant must have been a man of considerable strength as well.

"How's he holding up so far?" asked Detective Clark Johnson as he approached a tall, slender man sitting alone, smoking calmly, his eyes quietly scanning every movement inside Don Capaldo's opulent residence. "He's holding up... well, considering," replied Don Virginio De Palma, exhaling heavily. "He's in his room making phone calls. Doesn't want to be disturbed. Charlie was his only son. A terrible blow. To be honest, it hit me hard too. The kid was like a son to me; though I wish his father hadn't spoiled him so much, if you know what I mean." He offered the detective a cigarette.

"Yeah, I know exactly what you mean. No thanks, I quit." Detective Johnson paused. "We've made some progress in the investigation. That's something."

"You mean that whore you arrested?" Don De Palma asked bluntly.

"She's the key," said Detective Johnson. "She'll lead us to the killer. The guy was smart; didn't leave a trace, wiped every fingerprint, but that *girl* gave us a lead. The accomplice she mentioned works at *The New York Times*."

"What? You're telling me a journalist is involved?" Don De Palma said, astonished.

"No, no. Not a journalist. Just an office boy named Damien Todaro. But the bastard disappeared the moment the story broke," Detective Johnson clarified.

"Fucking press. Fucking media," Don De Palma muttered.

"Yeah, well, here's the thing, Virginio," the detective continued. "It's not just Damien who's missing. When we went to his workplace, we found out another guy, this one *is* a junior editor, vanished around the same time. Four days now, no word. Just like Damien."

"And what's the connection between this office boy and the missing editor?" Don De Palma asked.

"This editor isn't your typical employee. Turns out he's a bodybuilder; big, strong guy. We dug deeper and learned he also trains in a gym called Fury up in Chelsea, practicing something called MMA; Mixed Martial Arts, or whatever the fuck kids do nowadays..." Detective Johnson elaborated.

"Clark, what you're saying is nothing but bullshit! Yeah, I mean it; bullshit!" Don De Palma snapped. "There's no connection, no proof, just hearsay. Look, we need something solid, and fast. Carmine's not gonna stay calm much longer. We *need* to find who did this. What? Why are you looking at me like that, Clark?" Don De Palma demanded.

Detective Johnson met his eyes. "What if I told you I already know the kid who did it? I know him personally. Know his mother too. About four years ago, Charlie beat the hell out of this kid in Central Park. I went to the hospital as a favor for Nicky Glasses..."

"Wait, wait, hold on," Don De Palma cut him off. "Why the hell didn't you mention that before? And what's Nicky

Glasses got to do with this kid?"

"You think Carmine would've let Charlie face any consequences back then?" Detective Johnson shot back. "I'm the one who convinced the kid to drop the charges."

"And how would he even know who Charlie was unless *you* told him? You should've kept your fucking mouth shut, Clark!" Don De Palma barked.

The detective stiffened, stung by the rebuke. "You have no idea how furious they were, especially the mother. The boy needed surgery to repair the shoulder Charlie damaged. They were desperate to know who did it. If I hadn't helped, they'd have simply gone to someone else. Besides, Charlie wasn't exactly anonymous. Anyone could've recognized him from the description." Then Detective Johnson snapped. "Oh, don't give me that look, Virginio. Listen, I get that you and Carmine are drowning in grief, but let's be honest; Charlie wasn't exactly an angel. So, do me a favor, don't make him a martyr."

A heavy silence fell between them. Finally, Don De Palma broke it with a measured tone. "Is there anything else you can tell me about the investigation?"

Detective Johnson nodded slowly.

"I'm listening, Clark," said Don De Palma, leaning forward.

"There's mounting evidence against this kid named Robert Soleri. He's strong enough to do it, and more importantly, he's got motive," the detective explained, his tone sharp and knowing.

"Soleri... never heard that name before. Oh, wait." Don De Palma's brow furrowed. "There used to be a waiter named Robert Soleri at Denari's, back in the sixties. Yeah, I remember him; a nice guy. But... no, can't be related."

Detective Johnson gave a small, knowing smile. "You're right. That man was his grandfather; killed in Vietnam. And it's not just him. The boy's mother, Claudia, works at Denari's too; she's the manager. Or *was*. She's vanished, just like her son. I just came from there. I confronted Nicky, laid out the facts. When he tried to play dumb, I told him flat-out he could be charged with obstruction and making false statements. And if Carmine found out Nicky was hiding anything about the man who killed his son..." Detective Johnson shook his head. "He'd be in serious fucking trouble. But I believe Nicky; he doesn't know a damn thing. Claudia and her son Robert just disappeared."

Don De Palma was reticent for a long moment. "Is there more?" he asked warily.

Detective Johnson took a deep breath. "Yes... but I'm not sure..."

"What?! Come on, just spit it out, Clark!" Don De Palma impatiently said.

"Robert Soleri is the son of Vincent Corleone," Detective Johnson finally revealed the last dark secret he had been keeping up his sleeve.

Don De Palma's jaw dropped. His eyes widened. Before he could respond, a heavy, chubby figure appeared in the doorway; face pale, eyes blazing. The air in the room turned cold.

The man's voice was low but commanding: "Everyone out. Now."

Police officers, FBI agents, and Detective Johnson obeyed without hesitation.

When the room emptied, Don Carmine Capaldo turned to his old friend and said grimly, "We need to make a move. Right now."

Claudia and Robert Soleri arrived at Don Corleone's vast Texas estate right on time, having miraculously escaped the blazing inferno consuming New York. The sheer scale of the ranch, immense, fortified, and alive with movement, left both mother and son speechless. The mansion itself, sprawling across thirty thousand square feet, stood like a modern fortress of power and taste. Built in the style of a contemporary farmhouse with a central pitched roof, every element had been imported from Europe; most notably from Italy. Even the bricks bore the mark of Italian craftsmanship. Two magnificent marble statues, one of Julius Caesar and the other of Don Vito Corleone, stood proudly at the entrance, lending an air of imperial dignity to the estate. Perched atop one of the ranch's rolling hills, the mansion exuded an imposing elegance and grandeur. Below it stretched an immaculate expanse of emerald lawn, at the center of which a grand fountain sent water arching skyward, filling the air with calm and serenity. Encircling the property was a towering brick wall crowned with barbed wire, reinforced by cutting-edge electronic sensors and high-definition surveillance cameras. Yet the true guarantee of security came from the thousand soldiers stationed across the estate; men bound by unwavering loyalty to Don Corleone. They stood guard day and night, inside and out, ensuring no harm could come to their leader. The ranch itself was a self-contained world, dotted with smaller houses to accommodate the soldiers. Their lives revolved around discipline and devotion; training relentlessly, protecting their Don, and, when duty called, carrying out the Family's will against those who dared defy it. Few ever *left* the ranch. Perhaps it was obedience to the stern commands of Colonel Amari, their authoritative *officer*; or perhaps it was because within these walls they had found something the outside world could never offer: peace of mind, purity of spirit, and a deep sense of brotherhood and belonging.

Robert, Claudia, and Don Corleone spent the first three days at the mansion in near silence, each enveloped in a storm of anxiety. Anxiety over the police and FBI investigations into Charlie Capaldo's murder. Anxiety over the inevitable widening of the dragnet in search of the *killer*. Anxiety over the future Claudia had conscientiously planned for her only son, now jeopardized. Anxiety over the unpredictable reaction of a desperate, powerful man with nothing left to lose. However, on the fourth day, after dinner, Don Corleone summoned them to his study.

"I've been making and receiving exhausting calls for the past seventy-two hours," the Don said. "I've managed to put some pressure on the police and the Feds. But unfortunately, so far... it doesn't look good."

Claudia and Robert exchanged a wordless glance.

"Why did you do it, Robert? Why?" Don Corleone asked, voice low but firm.

"Why?!" Robert shot back, sardonic and defiant. "You think you're in a position to reprimand me, huh? To make any moral judgments?"

Claudia sensed the aggression in her son's tone; directed at the only man who could actually save them from the mess he had created. And most importantly, the man Robert was disrespecting was his father.

"Robert, this is your father," she said gently. "He is the only person willing to help us now and save us from the tough spot you put us in. So, the least you can do is show him respect."

"Respect... respect for who?!" Robert snapped. "For a man who abandoned his woman and son all these years?

And now you lecture me about the 'tough spot' I put us in? What about the tough spot *you* put me in, Mom?"

"Don't you ever speak to your mother like that!" Don Corleone interjected sharply. "You have no idea what she went through raising you alone!"

"You stay the hell out of this! It's *because of you* we're in this mess!" Robert yelled.

"Oh really? So, I'm the one who beat Charlie Capaldo to death, right? **RIGHT**?!" Don Corleone shouted.

"Vincent, what can you tell us about the investigations? The legal procedures?" Claudia tried to soften the tension, though she had dreaded this moment for over twenty years.

"I just told you, Claudia; it doesn't look good," Don Corleone bellowed. "They arrested the hooker your genius kid hired to trap Carmine Capaldo's son. She confessed there was another man; an office boy at *The New York Times* your son recruited."

Claudia clenched her teeth, shaking her head.

"Have they found Damien yet? The office boy?" Robert asked, guilt lacing his voice.

"No, but they certainly will. A warrant has been issued. And when they catch him, he's going to talk. He's not taking the fall for you," Don Corleone said bluntly.

"Can't you just do anything, Vincent? Please... my son..."

"I'm not a magician, Claudia! I can't fix all the shit your son did!" the angry Don yelled.

"Oh, so now I'm just her son? Let's go, Mom. We don't need to hear this. We don't need his help," Robert snapped.

"Wait, Robert..." Claudia began, only to be cut off by Don Corleone. "If you wanna leave, leave. Go on. You'll get caught sooner or later. You'll spend the rest of your miserable life behind bars with the worst kind of people. Even your mind can't imagine how bad it will get. And

Carmine? He won't hesitate to send someone after you. What?! You think you're tough enough to survive prison, or a war with him? Go ahead... leave."

Robert turned to his mother. "We don't need this man, Mom. We don't know him. We should leave now, and we will come up with another plan."

"Robert! Will you shut up?! Just shut the fuck up!" Claudia screamed. "You're still alive *because* of this man. Without him, you'd be dead. You're reckless, irresponsible, and so ungrateful! You have no idea the mess you're in!"

"So ungrateful?! You speak to me about recklessness?! About irresponsibility?!" Robert's voice shook with anger and hurt. "You have no idea what it's like not to know your father! To grow up thinking he abandoned you! And then, after twenty-two fucking years, a man appears out of nowhere, and you tell me this is my father, and I'm supposed to accept it, just like that?! You're mad at me for what I did to that asshole who assaulted and humiliated me for no reason whatsoever?! Well, guess what, Mom, I'm ten times mad at you for keeping my father from me all my life! If you truly loved me, you would've at least told me, and then let me *decide*... I had every right to know. And you deprived me of that right."

Claudia paused, tears in her eyes. "Alright, that's it. You know something? You are absolutely right. You do need a father," she said, leaving the study.

For a few minutes, silence filled the room. Robert panted, exhausted as if he had just fought five rounds in a UFC match. He was irate, lost, and heartbroken.

"You're a good talker," Don Corleone said finally, impressively calm.

Robert remained silent, still turned away.

"No, I mean it. You speak well. You're intelligent, persuasive. You're no meathead, that's for sure," Don Corleone continued, grinning. Then, in a playful gesture, he flexed his arms, showing off his strength, lowering and raising his biceps comically. Robert chuckled despite himself.

"You go to the gym? Dumb question... of course you do. Listen, I like you. I like how you carry yourself. That doesn't mean I approve of your actions; not morally. But it was idiotic. You just went too far, and now... you're in trouble; **big** trouble. But I like you. I like your character. And just as my grandfather used to say: 'Every man has one destiny.' You'll understand what that means when the time comes."

Don Corleone stepped closer, placing his hands on Robert's broad shoulders. To Robert's surprise, he could not resist the touch. A touch he had longed for all his life, despite his mother's endless devotion. "It's all fucked up... everything," Robert whispered. "I apologize for the trouble my mother and I caused. I thank you for your help. But I think we better leave. We don't wanna bring you more trouble with the police or Capaldo."

"I did not abandon you, Robert," Don Corleone said tenderly.

Robert bowed his head. Words failed him.

"I loved your mother," Don Corleone continued softly. "And I still do. I wanted to marry her. When she ended it, I didn't understand then, but I do now. I never gave up; we were forced apart. Over the years, I only managed to keep a very faint, distant connection. And she never mentioned you. She kept you safe, away from danger, hoping for a better life for you than she had. She did it out of love, not cruelty as you might think. I know what it's like to grow up without a father. Believe me, I can absolutely relate. But hey, look at you... you're in a better position than I was. Your mother made you who you are. Be grateful."

"What do you want from me, Mr. Corleone?" Robert asked, brokenhearted.

"I need you, Robert. I need you now more than anyone else in this world," Don Corleone replied.

"All my life, I always wanted to be a man of respect, to be admired by everybody, and sometimes even feared. But I never wanted that kind of *life* you're offering me now. Never...," Robert said, voice shaking, tears falling.

"All the wealth and everything I've built throughout all these years will vanish if you don't carry the legacy," Don Corleone said, voice softening. "You, Robert, are the hope for a better tomorrow. Rest assured, son, if I'd known anything about you, I would never have left you to think I abandoned you... never." He cupped Robert's face. "You are the son I've always dreamed of."

"Oh, Dad..." Robert cried, finally embracing the man he had longed to call father. The paradox of his emotions was profound; moments ago, he had hated the *man's* guts, and wanted to leave, but now... his heart melted. He had finally found the father he had always wanted; the role model, the protector, the true mentor. He had finally found trust, love, and most of all, steadfast guidance.

And who knows... Robert reflected inwardly. Perhaps this was the chance for the life he had always dreamed of; a life with two caring parents. But first, they had to act quickly; time was no friend.

While he methodically prepared for a quick, devastating strike against his archenemy, his longtime friend and de facto right-hand man laid a hand on the table and said softly, "Carmine, give it time. We need to think this through." He wore a dour expression and kept polishing his golden Beretta M9, in absolute disregard for the man's vain advice. "It's only a matter of time before the police catch that cocksucker Soleri," Don Virginio De Palma continued. "And who knows; they might as well nab that son of a bitch Vincent for harboring a fugitive."

Don Carmine Capaldo was silent for a heartbeat, then snapped, "You know something, Virginio? You're a fucking disgrace. You're a disgrace to the Mafia."

"Carmine, please, look at the big picture," Don De Palma begged. "Hear me out, then decide."

"There is no fucking big picture, Virginio!" Don Capaldo shot back. He stared at his friend with a mix of fury and grief. Don De Palma pressed on, desperately trying to pull him back from a path that would undoubtedly doom them both.

"You don't need to remind me that *we* settle our own scores," Don De Palma said. "I'm only saying look at it differently. The hooker they arrested already confessed; she named an accomplice, that office boy at *The New York Times*. Clark told me they're looking for him not just in New York but all over the country. He can't hide forever. It's only a matter of time. As for Robert Soleri, the police have searched and are still searching. There's no sign of him or his mother. Nicky Glasses claims he doesn't know where they are, and both Clark and I believe him. Turning up the heat on Nicky will only make things worse for us. I understand your agony. Charlie was your son, and I'm not asking you to forgo avenging him. Not at all. If you must go to war with Vincent Corleone, I'll back you 100%. I only ask: wait. Let things become clear, then we make the move." Don De Palma exhaled.

"Are you done?" Don Capaldo asked. His friend nodded. Don Capaldo drew on his cigar and spoke, his voice hollow with loss. "I appreciate your condolences, Virginio, but you'll never understand my agony; you have daughters. You never had a son. I know Charlie (R.I.P.) wasn't perfect, but at least he respected his father. Losing your only son is like losing hope for the future. He is the one who should've buried me, not the other way around."

"That's exactly my point, Carmine; you're taking this too personally." Don De Palma's voice was calm, in an attempt to mollify the bereaved father's sorrow.

Don Capaldo raised a hand. "Let me finish." He seemed pulled into a vortex of despair. "The hooker is dead. Slit throat in her cell last night. Guards took an hour to get to her. Damien, the office boy... my instincts tell me this wasn't personal for him. It was strictly business. And I don't even think he knew that editor planned to kill my son; otherwise he would've handled it differently. Whether that story about Charlie beating Soleri is true or not, I don't buy that Charlie's death was accidental. If Vincent's involved in anything, then it was definitely planned. And whether Vincent knew or not, he won't sit idle while his own son is in danger. He'll act, no doubt about it. Look, this man has been a thorn in our side for more than twenty-five years. If we don't strike now, it will be seen as a substantial sign of weakness, and then we'll be clobbered by everyone... As for Nicky Glasses... We found him outside his restaurant half an hour ago. Confirmation came just before you arrived. And I don't give a flying fuck about the heat from his death. He had to go. This Robert Soleri has to go. And Vincent Corleone also has to go. It's either me or them. And I swear to Christ, Virginio, if you cross me this time, I'll shoot you myself."

Don De Palma absorbed the words like a devastating blow. It was impossible to reason with Don Capaldo anymore. The fuse for a destructive war had been lit; the very war Don De Palma had always feared and worked to avoid at any cost. The families were at war, and nothing on earth would stop the coming bloodshed. Worst of all, Don De Palma found himself trapped between a huge rock and a very hard place, or rather, between loyalty and survival...

"Hello..."

"Hey, Damien. Is that you?"

"Who is this?!"

"It's me. Robert. Robert Soleri."

"You son of a bitch! You fucked me..."

At first, the call revolved around Damien's tirade of insults, each one hitting Robert like an explosive brick. An inexorable stream of expletives poured from Damien's mouth, his voice so loud it threatened to shatter Robert's eardrums. It was a one-sided conversation; a dialogue of the deaf. And after a very long five minutes of sustained rage, Damien finally paused long enough to hear Robert's proposition. Skeptical and wary, Damien still struggled to trust him, but options were scarce, and survival left him little choice.

"Hello?! Damien, are you still there?"

"Yes. I'm here. Robert."

"We need to be careful. Where are you staying? Are you with someone?"

"Yes, at a friend's place."

"Good. Does your friend have an email?"

"Yes."

"I'll send the address of my place there. Your email is probably compromised, and I'm not sure if your phone is tapped. Better safe than sorry. When you get the email, write down the details, then delete it. Follow the instructions exactly. Understood?"

"Yes, Robert. But what is this place?"

"The safest place you could ever be. Everything will be explained in the email. Trust me. And don't tell anyone. No one. No matter who. And again, delete the email; this is crucial."

"Yeah, I got it. Robert."

"Give me your friend's email."

"Hold on... it's tony_montana1983@yahoo.com."

"Interesting... Alright. See you."

Robert ended the call immediately, unwilling to prolong the tense exchange. Turning, he found Don Corleone standing in the doorway.

"That was Damien," Robert said casually.

"Yes, I heard. He seems *decent*, but that phone of his..." Don Corleone began, only to be interrupted.

"No, don't worry. He bought it before the *accident* to stay in touch with me. I made sure it wasn't registered in his name; precautionary. I never intended to drag him into all this," Robert explained.

Don Corleone snickered. "Remind me, Damien what?"

"Damien Todaro," Robert replied.

"Good," the Godfather nodded.

"Are you sure there's no problem bringing him here? I don't wanna impose," Robert said cautiously.

"By no means. Italians are always welcome here; the ones on our side, at least," Don Corleone replied with a hint of amusement.

"Oh, and Robert," the Godfather added, "take this. Put it by your bed. You never know when you'll need it."

"A bulletproof vest? Godfather, why?"

"For your safety. More important than the gun you carry," Don Corleone elucidated. "And how's the crash course with Colonel Amari?"

Robert sighed. "Progress... slowly."

"I know the colonel can be a pain in the ass, but he's good. Trust me, there's a lot you can learn from him," the Godfather said, smiling.

Robert hesitated, then asked, "You really think Carmine Capaldo will attack us here? This place is like a fortress; it'd be suicide."

Don Corleone gave him a fatherly look. "A clever enemy always surprises you. Never ever underestimate the unexpected." Before leaving, he added, "Oh, one more thing. From now on, everywhere, on the ranch or anywhere else, you identify yourself as Robert Corleone. This is not a request."

Two days later, the guards at the ranch gate reported to Don Corleone that a young man had arrived. Though they had been informed of his coming, the guards insisted on seeing his ID and gave him a thorough frisk.

"Is that him?" Colonel Amari asked bluntly.

The lead guard nodded. "Yeah, Colonel. Damien Todaro, as the ID states."

It was the capo himself who escorted Damien through the gates, bringing him to see the Godfather. Don Corleone had a strict rule: no newcomer could bypass inspection. He would not allow treacherous or subversive elements to infiltrate the family. Modest and fair as a leader, he, along with Colonel Amari, made it clear to everyone that traitors would find no mercy. Everyone already knew the cost of betrayal. One look from Don Corleone was enough to judge a man's character, to assess a soldier's worth. When the consigliere brought Damien into the Godfather's study, where Robert was also present, Don Corleone's eyes fell on the young man, and approval was instant. After a brief interview, conducted to assert his authority and demonstrate his infallible judgment, Damien Todaro was dismissed. The Godfather turned to Robert with pride. "Well, son, you didn't just turn out to be strong, smart, and articulate. You also happen to be an extraordinary judge of character."

He sold his business. He sold everything he owned, including the luxurious penthouse that had once been so close to his heart. He could no longer bear living there alone; every room, even every corner, reminded him of his son. He emptied his bank accounts, focused on one thing alone; amassing enough money to recruit an army. Through his extensive connections, he hired mercenaries from Mexico. Three weeks of grueling preparation followed, each day devoted to meticulously planning the assault against the Godfather, Don Vincent Corleone. He refused to leave anything to luck or fate, placing his trust entirely in the power he had painstakingly gathered; and in the element of surprise. Don Virginio De Palma had no choice but to follow his friend's lead. He, too, invested everything he had in the coming strike. Together, they spent day and night poring over maps and orchestrating what Don Carmine Capaldo would later call "the Hit of the Era." Yet even as they thoroughly planned, Don De Palma knew the truth: the brokenhearted father's quest was sheer lunacy; a desperate, last-ditch attempt to challenge the invincible Corleone. Don De Palma understood they had long passed the point of negotiation with the Godfather. He knew deep down that after all their arduous efforts, the odds of success were extremely slim; once the floodgates of blood were opened, only the victorious could close them. He knew, with grim certainty, that he and his lifetime friend were teetering on the edge of the precipice.

On Monday, July 23, 2007, a black Jeep Wrangler carrying two passengers in the backseat led a long convoy of trucks, ostensibly belonging to Texas' largest shopping center, The Galleria, for camouflage. Less than a mile from the Godfather's ranch, the lead vehicle came to a halt, ending a tense, two-hour drive. Three thousand masked men poured from the trucks, armed to the teeth with M4 Carbines fitted with telescopic sights and night-vision devices, and M203 grenade launchers with an effective range of 350 meters. Don Capaldo and Don De Palma marshaled their forces with ruthless precision. The commandos advanced on the ranch with terrifying speed and chilling professionalism, their movements fueled by vengeance, as if Charlie Capaldo himself were at their side. Sophisticated equipment allowed them to breach the petrifying electric fence that encircled the sprawling estate. The objective of this *cleverly* planned offensive was clear: devastate the Corleone army; catch them unprepared, sow chaos, and reduce them to disarray. Once their defenses crumbled, the vengeful father would have free rein; to hunt down the young man who had killed his son, and finally, to eliminate the old Godfather who had resisted expanding his empire and diversifying his interests for roughly three decades. And within ten minutes, they were on the brink of achieving their objective. Around 3 a.m., a thunderous blast rocked the entire ranch, followed by an incessant series of explosions. Don Capaldo's men were tearing through everything in their path; cars, trucks, even the soldiers' scattered quarters. All hell had broken loose. Claudia was paralyzed with fear. Don Corleone and Robert, however, remained composed. The Godfather had already prepared his son for a preemptive strike. Robert quickly strapped on his bulletproof vest, loaded his Heckler & Koch, and grabbed a couple of spare magazines, just in case. Don Corleone hesitated for a fraction of a second, his paternal instincts tugging at him, but Colonel Amari's commanding presence snapped him back to focus.

"Vincent, stay inside. Over a hundred men are guarding the mansion. Don't worry about Robert; I won't lose sight of him. I promise," Colonel Amari said with authority. Understandingly, Don Corleone nodded, though his fear for his son's life was palpable. Before Robert could protest, Colonel Amari's voice cut through: "No! You and Damien stay within two feet of me. And that's not even negotiable. Do you hear me, Robert?!"

"Take care of yourself, Robert. And you too, Damien," Don Corleone said fondly, while Claudia's panic threatened to overwhelm her. The Godfather bore her outrage, knowing full well that Colonel Amari's judgment and combat expertise made him more than capable of protecting them. Colonel Amari himself was ringed by at least two hundred soldiers, guarding the capo, Damien, and most importantly, the future leader of the family, Robert Corleone. Despite the chaos and heavy toll, hundreds already dead, Don Corleone knew Robert had to face this ordeal. Only by standing in the fire could his son earn the soldiers' respect, loyalty, and allegiance. Participation in this battle was not optional; it was essential. On the day Robert would assume the mantle of leadership, he could not be seen as a weakling. He had to prove himself, even in the midst of war.

As soon as Don Corleone apprised Colonel Amari of the latest developments, the latter grasped the full gravity of the situation. It was crystal clear; Don Carmine Capaldo's only way to settle the score with the Godfather was a direct assault on the ranch. A plan had been drawn up, and every preparation had been rigorously put in place. Colonel Amari devised a brilliant tactic; he would use the rough terrain of the ranch to deceive the enemy. The Corleone soldiers would be divided into six groups. Five of these groups, each consisting of 120 men, would take positions at the front, holding their assigned strongholds for as long as possible. Upon receiving Colonel Amari's order via walkie-talkie, only half of each group would retreat, while the remaining soldiers stayed behind to resist and provide covering fire until the second order arrived. These strongholds were strategically spread across the ranch to distract, exhaust, and most of all, confuse the attackers, no matter their numbers or strength. Every soldier was fully briefed on the withdrawal plan, which had to be executed with the utmost precision to minimize casualties. The goal of this maneuver was simple: make the enemy believe the Corleone army was collapsing; soldiers scattered, out of communication, and running out of ammunition. Retreating soldiers would move on foot, avoiding vehicles to prevent easy targeting, and lure the mercenaries toward the rallying point atop a hill roughly 600 yards from the mansion where Don Corleone and Claudia were taking refuge. At the rallying point, Colonel Amari had positioned twenty-five M134 Miniguns, ready to cut down the advancing enemy. The sixth group of the Corleone army remained hidden, armed with assault rifles, primed for a decisive counterattack. In addition, at least fifty soldiers carried FGM-148 Javelin fire-and-forget anti-tank missiles, prepared for any unforeseen threat. The esteemed capo left nothing to chance. In war, surprises were deadly, and he intended to be the one delivering them. And indeed, it worked. The enemy took the bait. The mercenaries chased the retreating Corleone soldiers; only to run headlong into what could solely be described as the wrath of God... In less than two minutes, the front lines of the aggressors were annihilated. And those who tried to flee were hunted down, cut down by the soldiers who had remained in their strongholds, waiting for Colonel Amari's second order. The battlefield had become a slaughterhouse; there was no mercy for anyone who dared escape. The war raged for approximately an hour, until the Corleone soldiers had completely annihilated the savage aggressors; Don Corleone took no prisoners. The cost, however, was staggering. Most of the outlying houses were reduced to flames. Corpses littered the ranch, and dozens more were wounded, some critically, requiring immediate hospitalization. Still, the Corleone losses did not exceed 150. It was, without exaggeration, a scene of absolute carnage.

The only tangible spoils the Corleones claimed were the enemy trucks; intact and swiftly confiscated. Most importantly, none of Don Capaldo's forces had come anywhere near the mansion. Colonel Amari, however, restrained any sense of triumph. He ordered his men to scour the ranch inch by inch, leaving no corner unchecked, ensuring every trace of danger had been fully eradicated. During the search, a light reconnaissance helicopter spotted a black Jeep speeding along the road, trying to flee. When the driver was ordered to stop, a frenzied passenger fired wildly from the window. A single rocket struck the vehicle, and in an instant, it was reduced to smoldering wreckage. The three inside were unrecognizable, charred beyond recognition. Hours later, once the ranch was confirmed secure, Don Corleone and Colonel Amari approached the burned-out Jeep. The driver's identity remained unknown, but the two rear passengers were unmistakable; recognized only by the Godfather, thanks to their distinctive shapes and the stark, almost grotesque contrast between them.

"Are those them?" asked the resourceful consigliere.

The Godfather nodded coldly, without a word.

CHAPTER NINE

LONG-AWAITED REUNION

On a relaxing Friday afternoon, with the sun sliding toward the horizon and warm slants of light cutting through the clear blue sky, he and his new *friend*, who would soon become his right-hand man, were practicing clay-pigeon shooting on the Corleone ranch. "Place your right cheek against the stock, use your upper body, not your arms, and follow the target no matter where it goes," Colonel Amari said, enthusiastically coaching Robert and Damien. "Another tip, Colonel? These plates are freaking fast," Damien snapped, frustration in his voice; Robert chuckled. "Well, Damien, if you keep your big mouth shut, I'll give you something new to work on," the consigliere retorted dryly. Robert, intrigued by the capo's tone, asked, curious: "You've had us doing this for almost a month. Is there still something about the sport we haven't learned yet?" Colonel Amari smirked. "There's always something new, Robert. Yes, skeet shooting. Like trap, you shoot singles or doubles, but from different angles and seven distinct stations. It demands lightning reflexes and absolute precision. Shotguns hold only two shells; if you take two targets at once you can't afford to miss. So, you two, especially you, Damien, better shape up, or I'm gonna kick your asses." They all burst out laughing.

They sat together in the mansion's tranquil garden, as if still the same harmonious couple who once walked side by side through Central Park twenty-three years ago. Back then, she had been an innocent young woman who knew little of life, love, or men. Yet she never forgot the words her mother, Maria, whispered to her before passing; a final plea to safeguard her honor. The tone, the trembling gravity of those words, had clung to her heart ever since. Claudia never hated her first and only love, Vincent Corleone. He was not some fleeting affair or casual memory; he was, and would always remain, something extraordinary to her. Their love had been real, sincere, and all-consuming. From the first glance, she knew. She had wanted to spend the rest of her life with him. But she was bound by a promise her mother had compelled her to make. And yet... love is stronger than all promises. Love transcends them; it teaches forgiveness, the grace to release the past, and the courage to hope for a better future. She tried, perhaps even succeeded, in leaving her beloved behind, severing every tie to protect herself and her kid. She could never forget how broken her father had been after his calamity with the police when she was just a child, nor how harshly society judged them for being poor, and Italian. Years later, when she saw her son lost and despairing as her father once was, she refused to abandon him. Through it all, she stood by Robert, helping him gather himself piece by piece and see college through to the end. And when she sensed that her protection was no longer enough, she refused to surrender again. Determined and unyielding, she vowed to do whatever it took to save him; to steer him toward the life she had always dreamed he would lead. In the end, Claudia knew that the significance of one's choices can only be seen in retrospect; no one connects the dots looking forward. Saving her son's future, revealing to him his true father after all these years, and guiding him toward the inner peace he had long sought; all of it confirmed that Vincent's return at this particular moment was not only the right decision, but perhaps the best one she had ever made.

Robert was overcome with euphoria as he watched his mother and father sharing coffee, talking softly, and smiling together. They looked perfect; radiant, content, complete. The sight of them was like a scene from an old, romantic film poster; tender, timeless, unforgettable. It was an image he had longed for his entire life. Life had not been kind to his mother. On the contrary, it had been unforgivingly severe. From a young age, she had shouldered burdens far beyond her years; responsibilities that stole from her the chance to simply live, to enjoy, to be young. That truth had always broken Robert's heart. His mother was a remarkable woman, and she deserved so much more than hardship. All he had ever wanted was to see her safe, at peace, and above all, in love. So, when he saw the glow of happiness on his mother Claudia's face that afternoon, Robert smiled from the depths of his soul. That long-awaited joy, one he had thought impossible, had finally found her. It had taken nearly a quarter of a century for that dream to come true, but as the saying goes, *better late than never...*

"Hello, are the laborers still here?" Robert asked his parents.

"Yeah," Claudia replied calmly. "They're still repairing the damage from that night."

Most of the soldiers' houses had been severely vandalized and now needed complete reconstruction.

Robert let out a deep sigh, fully aware of the impact his words would have on his parents, especially his mother, but he needed to get them off his chest. "You know, after this nightmare is over at last, I must admit... I miss Nicky very much. He's the only person I truly wish could be here with us today. He would have been so happy to see you two finally together..."

Claudia bowed her head, tears welling in her eyes.

"There's a letter for you, Robert," said the Godfather, handing his son a sealed envelope in an attempt to shift the conversation and lighten the mood.

"A letter? For me? In *this* era? Hmmm... interesting," Robert remarked with a hint of humor, while his parents exchanged a silent glance. He excused himself politely and made his way to Don Corleone's study for a moment of privacy. Sitting down in the chair that had once belonged to his great-grandfather, he carefully slit open the envelope with an elegant wooden letter opener.

Dear Robert,

I hope this letter finds you safe and well.

I must have thought a thousand times before deciding to write it, for many reasons. I know how upset you were, and probably still are, with me after that night. It turned out it wasn't just you. Your mother was angry with me too. I liked her very much, but sadly we lost touch right afterward. I wasn't really sure whether you would even appreciate this gesture. After all, writing letters feels almost obsolete these days, but I don't have your new email address. I found your current home address through the stories in the newspapers and online about what happened at your father's ranch in Texas. Most importantly, I'm by no means a skilled writer, and even if I were, I could never hope to match your remarkable eloquence or your gift with words.

And, last but certainly not least, my terrible handwriting, as you well know...

You are truly a special person, Robert, special in every sense of the word. No, I really mean it. You're handsome, intelligent, accomplished, thoughtful, witty, and, surely most endearingly, deeply romantic. Don't think for a moment that I didn't cherish what you said to me that night. Do you remember when you asked why I ended our relationship so abruptly? I couldn't give you an answer then, not because I didn't care, but because I honestly didn't have a clear one. There was something about you I felt deeply, something I couldn't quite explain. I know this must feel awkward for you now. You're probably asking yourself: "What the hell does she want from me? Why is she writing me after all this time? Has she lost her mind?"

The truth, Robert, is that I love you. I love you deeply, more than I have ever loved, or ever will love, anyone. Everything about you makes it impossible not to. But by now, I believe you understand why I chose to end it. I don't want to intrude or meddle in matters that are no longer mine to touch. You don't owe me, or anyone else, an explanation. And I am positive that someone as perceptive as you understands what I meant when I said you weren't the right man for me, or the right father for my children. I ended it, Robert, because I took you seriously, perhaps even more seriously than you took me. And because I saw no future for us, I ended it before our beautiful story could turn into something painful.

Still, I'll always be grateful for what we shared. I wish you nothing but happiness, and I have no doubt that God will bring into your life the woman you've long been searching for, the one worthy of the love you carry within you.

With all my heart,
Judith Eisenberg

After reading the final line, Robert lingered for a moment, his eyes fixed on the handwriting as if it still carried her voice. Then, with deliberate calm, he reached for the golden Zippo. The flame flickered to life, its glow dancing against the polished wood of the desk. He touched it to the edge of the letter. The paper caught quickly, curling in on itself, the ink dissolving into smoke and memory. As the last fragments turned to ash in the tray, a glint from the mirror drew his gaze. For an instant, he saw a reflection, strange, almost otherworldly, yet, to his surprise, he found it... congenial.